Scottish
Bakehouse
Mysteries™

Of Ice and Men

Elizabeth Penney

Annie's®
AnniesFiction.com

Books in the Scottish Bakehouse Mysteries series

Of Ice and Men
Copyright © 2020 Annie's.

Library of Congress-in-Publication Data
Of Ice and Men / by Elizabeth Penney
p. cm.
I. Title
              2020940197

AnniesFiction.com
(800) 282-6643
Scottish Bakehouse Mysteries™
Series Creator: Shari Lohner
Series Editor: Elizabeth Morrissey
Cover Illustrator: Kelley McMorris

10 11 12 13 14 | Printed in China | 9 8 7 6 5 4 3 2

1

"Would you look at that?" Carol MacCallan asked, a note of awe in her voice. Her hands stilled on the stack of plates she was unloading from a tray. "I guess the forecasters were right."

Molly Ferris followed her friend and business partner's gaze to the tall windows of the old Victorian that housed Bread on Arrival, their Scottish bakehouse. If the precipitation were rain, she'd say it was bucketing down. But it was dense, heavy snowflakes that made it nearly impossible to see more than a few feet into an almost impenetrable veil of white.

Molly shivered as a gust of wind buffeted the building. "I heard it's the worst winter in fifty years. And it's only January." Even to her own ears, her laugh sounded a little frantic. Moving automatically, she scooped coffee into a filter and slid it into the machine, then pressed the button. She'd lost count of the number of pots she'd brewed today.

Fortunately, the weather wasn't keeping customers away. No, they seemed as desperate as Molly felt to relieve the season's monotony by getting out of their homes for a while. They liked sitting by the roaring fire, sipping hot drinks, and devouring delicious baked goods created by Laura Donovan, the third partner in what had come to be known as the Bakehouse Three. The women had been roommates in college, and their friendship had endured more than three decades—long enough to decide they all wanted to try their hands at a midlife career shift into bakehouse ownership, which had come along with a move to the quaint Scottish-themed town of Loch Mallaig in Michigan's Upper Peninsula.

"Are ye suffering from a wee bit of cabin fever, perhaps?" part-timer Hamish Bruce inquired. He stroked his white beard, blue eyes twinkling as he exaggerated the faint Scottish burr he had acquired as a lifelong resident of Loch Mallaig. "You're as fidgety as Octavius and June."

As a matter of fact, Molly did empathize with Hamish's pet budgies. Their cage was large and well-appointed, but it was still a cage. "Do you blame me?" She made a dramatic gesture. "I not only work here, but I live upstairs. I haven't been anywhere for a week." If not for needing groceries or walking Angus, her Scottish terrier, she wouldn't even have put her nose outside during this last cold snap. Having grown up in Ann Arbor, Molly had endured many a Michigan winter, but this year seemed a bigger struggle than ever.

"You're not the only one who's getting edgy," Carol said. She put a Scottish snowball on a plate and set it in front of Molly. "Harvey's been climbing the walls. Thank goodness the Jock McCauley Ice Fishing Derby is starting today and lasts into next week."

"That seems like a long time for a fishing tournament," Molly mused.

Carol laughed. "The entrants are a bunch of bored retirees and guys who do warm-season work like construction. They'd let it last two months if they could."

"Are they actually ice fishing today in this storm?" Molly held up the confection, a raspberry sandwich cookie dipped in powdered sugar and coconut. "These are the only snowballs I want to see." She took a bite, allowing the sweetness of sugar and vanilla to mingle on her tongue with the slightly tart raspberry.

"Apparently so," Carol said. "If the snow backs off, I plan to go down to the loch later and check it out."

"Take me with you," Molly practically begged. "Angus will enjoy the outing too. One good thing about his black fur—we won't lose him in the snow." Molly's spirits lifted, although she didn't know if it was the sugar boost or the mild joke.

The front door opened to admit Fergus MacGregor, owner of the Castleglen golf resort and lodge. He stamped his snowy feet on the doormat and said, "It's a good day for polar bears." He pulled off a knit cap to reveal dark, tousled hair that he straightened with his fingers, then stuffed the cap into his parka pocket.

At the sight of her friend, Molly's spirits lightened further. "Welcome," she called, waving her half-eaten snowball. "You've got to try one of these."

"Way to market our goodies," Laura said with a laugh, carrying a tray of buttery melting moments to the case.

"Molly's method might have serious consequences for our waistlines," Carol said wryly. "And it's tough enough to keep the pounds off in winter anyway." Strong and fit thanks to her regular Pilates sessions and the fact that she was on her feet at the bakery all day, Carol's concerns were likely misplaced.

"You look wonderful, Carol," Fergus said gallantly. He pointed at the snowball. "I'd like to try one of those and the largest coffee you can pour." He rubbed his hands together. "It's brisk out there."

Molly hurried to do the honors. "How are the roads?"

Fergus made a face. "A little slick. And this last squall came so suddenly that the plow trucks haven't been able to keep up."

As if summoned by his words, a large orange truck, its lights flashing, went past on the road with an audible scrape of the huge plow. *The soundtrack of winter,* Molly thought. She could be anywhere and she would recognize that sound.

"There they go," Hamish said. "I'm sure they'll be working 'round the clock. Again."

Laura, who had been assessing the cookies remaining in the case, finished and stood. "I'll have to make up a box of goodies for the public works employees. They deserve a treat."

Fergus sipped from the coffee Molly had poured, lingering by the counter while she rang up the sale. "I'll drop it off on my way home if you want."

"How nice," Carol said. "I'm going to take some treats and hot drinks out to the ice fishermen later."

"I love that idea," Molly said. "I'll help. We'll carry twice as much with the two of us."

"Perfect." Carol smiled, then cocked her ear toward the sound of a timer going off in the kitchen.

"Duty calls." Laura gave a salute, then hustled away.

"So Harvey is still doing the tournament today?" Fergus asked, returning his wallet to his pocket. "I know he'll fish in any weather, but this is something else."

Carol snorted. "Of course he's still doing it. He's been talking about it for weeks, hoping the ice would cooperate and freeze deep enough."

"It's thick enough for sure." Even though Fergus had his order, he didn't seem eager to leave the counter and go sit down. "I was there when they cut a test section. It's over a foot deep."

Hamish folded the newspaper he'd been leafing through. "Enough to hold a vehicle then. If it's over eight inches, you can drive on it with a small car. Trucks, you need fifteen inches at least." The retired history teacher was a font of information about the most eclectic matters.

"They're using snowmobiles to pull the bob-houses out, so they should be all right," Carol said. "But now they have extra snow to dig through to make their fishing holes."

"A lot of it blows off," Fergus said. "You'd be surprised." He took another sip of coffee. "Anyway, it's a nice memorial event for Jock. It even starts on his birthday."

"Did you know him?" Molly asked.

Fergus smiled. "I sure did. Jock McCauley was a great old guy. It's too bad he passed before you moved to town."

Molly leaned on the counter. "He was the original owner of Neeps and Tatties, right?"

"That's right," Fergus confirmed. "Brodie McCauley is his nephew. The food now is every bit as good if not better, though that could be Catriona's influence."

"Between Brodie's family recipes and his wife being a trained chef, I'm not surprised," Molly said, suppressing a giggle as Fergus took a bite of the snowball and shed coconut all over his short beard.

"I'm looking forward to the Burns Week kickoff dinner the historical society is holding at Neeps and Tatties," Carol put in, then chuckled. "My grandkids are jealous that Robert Burns gets a whole week to celebrate his birthday, instead of only one day—especially since the twins have to share a birthday. Try explaining to seven-year-olds the importance of Scotland's premiere eighteenth-century poet."

"I wouldn't know how to begin," Molly said, laughing. "Now that I think of it, I'm surprised the derby and the birthday celebration are being held at the same time." She raised an eyebrow, thinking of the town's head librarian, who was also the Burns event's chief planner. "Usually Grizela Duff doesn't like competition."

"Ah, but Grizela has a soft spot for poetry lovers," Fergus replied. "She and Jock were friends, and she knows he was a huge fan of Burns. He would have gotten a kick out of the derby and the birthday celebration coinciding."

Squaring his shoulders, Hamish began to recite, exaggerating the natural Scottish brogue he shared with many other Loch Mallaig residents. "'The wintry west extends his blast.'"

Fergus joined in with the next line. "'And hail and rain does blaw; Or, the stormy north sends driving forth the blinding sleet and snaw.'"

The men gave a bow as their recital concluded, drawing a few claps from around the room. Fergus still had flakes of coconut in his beard, and they resembled snowflakes to Molly's amused eyes.

Fergus grinned at Molly. "I can keep going if you want. I had to memorize the whole poem for a class."

"That's a nice offer," Molly said. "But I've got a feeling we'll have lots of opportunities to hear Burns verses this week."

"But boy, talk about a perfect poem for today." Carol gestured toward the window. "From what I've heard, the weather in Scotland can get nasty too."

"I think they get snow, but not as much as us," Molly said glumly. "I wouldn't mind if we'd had a white Christmas and a green New Year."

"Cheer up, lass," Hamish said, clearing a nearby table with a clatter of dishes. "Life's too short to get down in the mouth."

Molly fixed an amazed stare on Hamish. Normally he was a grumbling bear of a man making a fuss about the smallest inconveniences.

Before she could comment, he went on. "Are the Snide Pipers playing during this week's festivities?" he asked, invoking one of his nicknames for the local bagpipe group Molly played in. "I can hardly wait."

There's the Hamish I know and love. Molly raised her head with dignity. "Yes, The Piping Yoopers are playing. And Bridget is dancing with The Leaping Lowlanders," she added, knowing the mention of sunny Bridget Ross, the bakehouse's other part-timer, would soften Hamish. Everyone loved Bridget.

"Speaking of the festivities," Fergus said, "are you going to the planning committee meeting tonight, Molly? I am."

"Wouldn't miss it," she told him.

"Me neither," Carol chimed in. "Grizela would kill me." Grizela ran a tight ship, both at the Loch Mallaig Library and as the president of the historical society.

Laura emerged from the kitchen, holding a large bakery box. She set it on the counter and patted the top. "This is for the public works department. Thanks again for delivering it, Fergus."

"No problem." Fergus popped the last of the snowball into his mouth and drained his coffee. "I hate to eat and run, but I've got to get back to the resort. See you tonight, ladies." He nodded farewell to Hamish, and exited into the teeth of the snow squall.

But as Molly watched him drive his silver Range Rover out of the lot, she saw a patch of blue appear in the sky, as if the clouds had been torn apart. The snowfall lightened, tapering off as fast as it had started, and shafts of sunlight warmed the bakehouse floors. They had a reprieve . . . for the moment.

Perhaps lured out by the sunshine, customers streamed in at a steady pace for the rest of the morning and afternoon. Molly finally took a much needed break and ran upstairs to her apartment. Even before she got the door open, she heard Angus snuffling at the threshold, nails dancing on the wood floor.

"Hold on, hold on," she said with a laugh when she got inside. "Don't worry. We're taking a walk."

She dressed him in a warm coat—red with white snowflakes on it—then put on her own winter gear: lined boots, a puffy down parka, wool hat, and fur-lined gloves. She felt as round and soft as a marshmallow, but she was taking no chances with Michigan winter. Not wanting to brave the outside steps, which could be slippery, she went down the inside staircase and out through the back door.

Angus spent plenty of time in the fenced backyard during the day, but that didn't give Molly any exercise, so she forced herself to get out at least once a day and stretch her legs. Although she was on her feet much of the time in the bakehouse, it wasn't the same as a brisk stroll in fresh air.

Very fresh air today, Molly mused as the breeze slapped her cheeks. She and Angus entered Dumfries Park, where the wonderful public works department kept the main paths clear of snow all winter. Otherwise, no one could use the trails until spring.

At first Molly thought she and Angus were alone, but then she saw a figure running in the distance. A jogger, judging by the way the person pumped his or her fists. She'd always admired but never shared the dedication of runners who braved the worst weather conditions for strenuous exercise.

The jogger turned a corner and headed toward Molly, still moving fast. Build and height revealed the runner was male. A hat worn low over the brow and a half mask hid his facial features—but they couldn't conceal the glare in his ice-blue eyes.

The sense of barely checked rage was so fierce, Molly recoiled. However, it seemed the runner's anger wasn't directed at her. He swept past, ignoring Angus's adorably longing gaze, and was gone. But he left a lingering swirl of dark energy in his wake.

The short winter day was slanting toward evening when Molly and Carol drove out to the ice fishing tournament. The event was being held on Loch Mallaig's namesake lake in front of Castleglen, so to access it, they drove past the main lodge and down to the shorefront. In summer, this was a lively scene of swimmers, fishermen, and kayakers, but today there was only the huddle of bob-houses set a distance from the shore.

"Are we taking the refreshments out to the bob-houses?" Molly asked. In addition to the baked goods, they'd brought large insulated pots filled with coffee and hot chocolate.

"No, thank goodness," Carol said with a laugh. "We're going in here." She parked in a lot beside a tidy, whitewashed cottage used as a changing house and concession stand in the warmer months. Lights were on in the interior of the cottage and a stream of smoke drifted from the chimney. Harvey's truck was parked along with several other cars that probably belonged to the other fishermen.

Although Molly would have liked to walk out on the lake and visit Harvey's fishing hut, she didn't mind that they'd be inside the warm cottage. The snow had stopped for now, but as the sun sank, so did the temperature.

They headed along a shoveled path to the front of the house, Carol carrying the box of baked goods and Molly toting the insulated pots. As they came around the corner, Molly saw a group of men standing on and near the porch, where a hanging scale was set up. A large fish with mottled skin rested in the weigh basket, hanging out on both ends.

The activity around the weigh station was interesting, but what caught Molly's eye was a big, burly man with his fist raised, who was advancing on a much slighter man. Two equally large men stood poised behind the aggressor, as if to provide backup.

Had Molly and Carol walked in on a brawl in the making?

2

Carol's steps hitched. "What's going on?" She craned her neck, scanning the onlookers. "There's Harvey."

Molly spotted Harvey's friendly, handsome face at the fringe of the crowd. To be honest, she spotted his red plaid tam with its big pom-pom first. Carol had bought him that hat in Scotland, and he wore it a lot.

As they drew closer, the snatches of words they caught on the wind resolved into intelligible sentences. "Hold on a moment," the slighter man said. His tone was deep and rich, what some might call a radio voice. "As judge of this contest, I am responsible for ascertaining the source of each entry so as to ensure the utmost—"

The man who had been shaking his fist interrupted with a bark of laughter. "Enough already. You accused me of cheating by catching a bigger, heavier fish somewhere else and bringing it here." He thumbed his chest. "I heard you. And my friends heard you."

"That's right, you did," one of the friends said. "And Rick here heard it too. Didn't you, Rick?" The third man nodded.

A young man spoke up. "I'm sorry about this misunderstanding. Why don't we go ahead and enter your catch?" He stepped to the scale, and something about the way he moved seemed familiar to Molly.

She squinted at him. Could he be the runner she'd seen earlier? He didn't seem at all angry now. In fact, he was being rather ingratiating to the angry fisherman, sending him conciliatory smiles every few seconds as he weighed the fish.

"This sure is a big one," the younger man said, steadying the scale basket. "A real beauty."

Crunching footsteps sounded behind Molly, and she turned to see who was coming. Rail-thin Vernon Pennycook, owner of The Auld Crabbit bait shop, was trudging along, eyes glowering under his thick brows. It wasn't surprising that he was here, since he was one of the most avid fishermen in Loch Mallaig—and notoriously one of the grouchiest residents. When he got really fired up, he made Hamish seem like a cuddly old teddy bear.

"Hello, Vernon," Molly said. "Here for the tournament?"

His response was a grunt. "I'm in charge, aren't I?" He continued slowly but surely toward the group, his shoulders hunched over with age.

Relief broke across the young man's face when he saw Vernon. "Hey, boss. Glad you made it back. We're weighing up today's catches." He lifted the fish from the scale using two hands. "Check out this beauty." He placed it gently on the table and began to measure its length from head to tail.

Vernon's gaze roamed the crowd. "Och, looks like ye all had a fine day." He trudged over to one of the people waiting to have his fish weighed and asked to see his catch. They were soon deep in conversation about fishing exploits.

The expert fisherman's presence appeared to calm the troubled waters of the situation. Even the burly trio seemed mollified. Carol and Molly continued toward the cottage, joined by Harvey, who cut through the throng to meet them.

After greeting the women, he reached for Carol's box. "Let me take that," he said, then nodded his head at another man to indicate he should come take Molly's burden.

The foursome climbed the porch steps and went inside. All was warm and toasty in the cottage, with a large cast-iron woodstove radiating heat, the flames visible through glass doors. The cottage had one main room with benches lining the walls and a couple of long tables in the middle. Doors on either end led to the men's and women's restrooms and changing areas, while in the back, a pass-through window was open to reveal a kitchen beyond.

Harvey set the box on the table, where there were already cups, plates, and napkins, and his companion did the same. "Thanks, Sheldon," Harvey said. "Do you know my wife, Carol, and her friend, Molly Ferris? Ladies, this is Sheldon Barker."

Sheldon, who had wind-reddened cheeks and seemed to be in his forties, grinned. "I haven't had the pleasure." He pulled off a glove and extended his hand. "Nice to meet you both."

"Are you a visitor to Loch Mallaig?" Carol asked politely as they all removed their coats and hung them on a rack.

"The wife and I recently moved here from Marquette," Sheldon said, edging closer to the warm fire and rubbing his hands together. "I'm in insurance, with my own agency." He eyed Molly. "In fact, if you need—"

Guessing he was about to launch into a sales pitch, Molly interrupted, "Would you like a cup of coffee?" She pulled a cup off the stack and held it poised under the spigot. "Fresh brewed right before we left Bread on Arrival."

"I can't say no to that." Sheldon left the stove and ambled over to the table. After Molly dispensed the coffee, he moved along to the cream and sugar that Carol had set out.

"What was all that about outside?" Carol asked Harvey as she opened the lid of the pastry box. "I thought that fisherman was going to punch the judge." She glanced out the window. "And who is the judge this year? I didn't recognize him."

Molly poured a cup of coffee for Harvey. "I didn't either. Is he another newcomer?"

Harvey took the coffee with a smile of thanks. "Finlay Croft is his name. A friend of his has a cabin here, so he's been coming up quite often. They're both professors at Barrie-Firth College." Harvey added cream and sugar to his coffee, stirring it thoroughly.

Sheldon perked up. "Barrie-Firth? That's in my old neck of the woods. Good college."

Harvey acknowledged this contribution with a nod. "Anyway, Vernon was looking for another judge this year because he wanted to cut back. He's been organizing and judging the derby since it started. Finlay offered, and that was that." He shrugged. "Most of us want to fish, not judge."

Carol straightened the collar of Harvey's plaid flannel shirt. "How did you do today, dear?"

Her husband made a face. "Nary a bite. But there's always tomorrow."

"Good thing, huh?" Sheldon barked a laugh. "I'm in the same boat. Or actually not, at this time of year, but you know what I mean."

Molly gave his joke a polite smile. "Better luck tomorrow, then. Both of you."

Carol sat on a bench, stretching her legs out. "So what happened with the argument?" Harvey and Molly joined her, but Sheldon remained standing near the stove.

Harvey's lips twisted in a grimace. "Finlay accused Sam of cheating by bringing in a fish he caught elsewhere."

"That sure was a big pike, you have to admit," Sheldon said with a whistle. "Going to be a hard one to beat."

"Well, for me, it's more about the chase than the actual catch," Harvey said. "If we depended on fishing to eat, well, that might be a different story."

"Yes," Carol agreed. "Thank goodness for the grocery store."

Harvey's attitude was a healthy one, Molly reflected. But for some people, competition wasn't fun unless they were winning. She scanned the contest flyer pinned to the wall nearby. Whoever took first place would win a hefty cash prize. She didn't know much about fishing, but Molly guessed it would pay for a lot of equipment.

"Do you want to walk out and see Harvey's bob-house before we go?" Carol asked Molly. "We won't linger. It's too cold."

Outside, the winter sun was dipping low, casting blue shadows, but it couldn't be any worse than the walk she'd taken earlier. "I'm game," Molly said. "I've always been intrigued by bob-houses. They're cute."

While she was sliding her coat back on, Molly saw a slender woman with a sharp nose and a sour expression outside. She wore a quilted parka and a fur-lined hat with flaps. She spoke to someone and they pointed toward the cottage.

The woman stomped up the porch steps and came inside. Molly had to step aside quickly to avoid the swinging door. "There you are," the woman said to Sheldon, her voice as sour as her face. "I thought you'd be home by now."

Sheldon gave a nervous laugh. "I was about to leave. You didn't need to venture all the way out here." He tossed his empty cup into a trash can.

The woman pulled her hat off with her left hand, revealing a head of blonde curls. "Oh, it's not far." She turned to the others. "We live on Bridgegate Drive."

"My friend Laura lives on Bridgegate too," Molly said. "Hers is the original crofter's cottage for the Castleglen estate. Fortunately, it's been kept up well."

"Small world. Ours is brand new, though. Probably a little less drafty." The woman smiled thinly for a moment, then refocused on

Sheldon. "I'm going to head back out," she said, then added pointedly, "There's a big pile of customer paperwork for you to go over at home."

"Be there in ten, honey." After the woman left the cottage, Sheldon explained, "That's my wife, Sheila. She helps me in the office." He gave an uneasy chuckle. "And, as you can see, she has her moods."

No one had a response to this observation, and after a moment, Harvey heaved himself to his feet. "See you tomorrow, Sheldon. Have a good night."

"You too." Sheldon glanced at Molly and Carol. "Nice meeting you. Thanks for the coffee." He zipped up his coat, then left.

As Molly stepped out of the cottage with Harvey and Carol a couple of minutes later, a group of fishermen passed them going up the steps. Through the big front window, she saw them cluster around the table, eagerly helping themselves to goodies and hot drinks.

Vernon and Finlay were talking near the weigh station while the younger man cleaned up the area. "Next time you think there's a problem with the catch," Vernon told the judge, "Come get me." He made a snorting sound. "I've been fishing on the loch so long I practically *ken* all the fish by name. I'll be able to tell if one of 'em came from somewhere else." At this remark, the younger man smiled to himself.

Finlay stood with arms folded across his chest, his expression both condescending and skeptical. "If you insist. But there was something shifty about those fellows. And Jeanne says—"

"How is Jeanne?" Vernon interrupted. "I haven't seen her yet." He nodded at Molly and the others. "Giving them the grand tour, Harvey?"

"I am," Harvey said with his rich chuckle. "They think the bob-houses are cute."

This remark was met with laughter from Vernon and the young man, while Finlay merely seemed bored at this diversion of the conversation.

"They're cute enough when you need one," Vernon agreed. "They keep the wind off your back at least."

With Harvey leading the way, Carol and Molly trudged along a well-worn path through the snow to the shore. On the lake itself, other tracks led to the various houses set a short distance apart from each other.

"Who is the young man helping with the weighing?" Molly asked. "I don't think I've met him."

"That's Noah Taggart," Harvey said. "He works for Vernon at the bait shop."

Harvey led them to the bob-house on the end, a little square structure with windows on each side and a door in front. It sat on runners that allowed it to be pulled onto the lake by a snowmobile.

"Welcome to my humble abode," Harvey said, opening the door and standing back to let the women enter first. "Emphasis on the humble."

There was barely enough room for all three of them in the shack, which was furnished only with benches around the walls and a small propane heater. A couple of circular holes were cut in the wood floor, and matching openings were carved into the ice below.

"Those are my fishing holes," Harvey said. "I cast my lines into the water, and I drink coffee and think about life until something bites. It's not a bad pastime."

"Especially when you bring something home." Carol turned to Molly. "He tosses back most of his catches, but once in a while, he keeps a fish for us to enjoy."

Molly sat on a bench, picturing herself ice fishing. It really was peaceful out here on the ice, and the windows were at the right height to enjoy the scenery.

"Some fellows bring radios or televisions," Harvey said, "but I think that defeats the whole point. You go fishing to get away from all that."

As if the world was reminding them it really hadn't gone away, Molly's phone rang in her pocket. She considered ignoring it and wished she'd at least put it on silent.

"You'd better get that," Carol said. "It might be important."

Molly dug the phone out of her coat pocket right before it went to voice mail. "Hello?"

"Molly?" It was Laura. "Sorry to bother you, but Grizela called right as I was leaving the bakery. She said there's a big problem with the Burns Week."

Uh-oh. "What is it?" Molly asked. Everyone had worked so hard to pull the event together. They certainly didn't need a last-minute problem.

"The orator canceled," Laura explained. "Not only does he have a bad cold, but there's a blizzard grounding planes in Chicago."

Molly gasped. "What are we going to do? Without an orator to recite Robert Burns poetry, our celebration is ruined."

Laura sighed. "Maybe Grizela will think of something. She's changed tonight's planning meeting to an emergency strategy session."

"We'll be there," Molly said glumly. She disconnected, her sense of relaxation gone as she filled in Carol and Harvey, who groaned in dismay. "I guess we'd better get going. Sounds like tonight's meeting isn't going to be much fun."

"Oh well," Carol said. "It can't be helped. I sure hope we can salvage the event."

Harvey put a hand on his chest. "I'll be the orator." He cleared his throat then intoned, "'Ae fond kiss and then we sever; Ae fareweel, alas for ever.'" His voice was wonderful to listen to, but something about his inflection was a bit off.

Carol and Molly exchanged glances. "Honey, you know I love you," Carol said hesitantly.

"But I stink." Harvey blew air out through his lips. "I know. But I thought I'd at least try to help you out."

Molly stood. "And we appreciate it, honestly." She stamped her feet to get the blood moving again.

"Maybe we should ask Hamish to do it," Carol said. "Or Fergus. They both sounded great this morning reciting that bit of poetry."

"They did," Molly agreed. "But somehow I don't think either of them is ready for a stage debut. The orator is going to perform every night of the event, almost as if he's playing the role of Robert Burns."

"True," Carol said. "And they don't have much time to memorize the poetry."

Molly sighed. "I'm not going to panic yet. I'm sure we'll be able to come up with a plan."

"I sure hope so," Carol said, standing up too. "Or we'll have a week's worth of haggis to eat."

"Haggis?" Harvey's brows rose at the mention of the traditional Scottish dish. "Now there's a meal that will put hair on a man's chest."

"A main part of our preparations was coming up with elaborate meals worthy of Robert Burns," Molly explained. "Haggis is playing a starring role at the first event, a traditional Burns supper. It will be brought in to much fanfare."

"Can't wait." Harvey gestured to the doorway. "Shall we?" He followed them out of the hut, then locked the door.

The trio trudged across the snow-covered ice to the shore, where they parted ways. Harvey promised to grab the beverage containers and bring them home after the tournament disbanded for the night.

The flurries started again as Carol drove along the quiet roads. Evening settled around them and lights glowed in the homes they passed, warm and cheerful.

While Molly appreciated the cozy scene, she couldn't help but wonder. How would she make it until spring? The infamous UP winter had barely begun, and it looked like they were in for a "joyless winter day" indeed, as Burns called it—or a string of them.

Back at her apartment, Molly ran a hot bath. Even that brief excursion to the lake had chilled her to the bone. But lounging in lavender-scented bubbles helped, as did the plate of homemade macaroni and cheese she heated up for dinner.

"The ultimate comfort food," she told Angus between mouthfuls. He whined and stared at her hopefully, wanting in on this treat. "Oh Angus. You're such a pro at laying on the guilt."

She got up and gave him a biscuit from the treat cabinet. He padded over to his bed to crunch on it contentedly.

Molly dressed warmly in wool slacks and a sweater, dreading the thought of going out into the cold again. But the thick, knitted socks on her feet and her plush shearling-lined boots made her feel a little better. "I'll be back later, buddy," she told Angus, who was sound asleep in his bed.

The meeting was at the library on Balmoral Lane, just far enough away that Molly decided to drive rather than walk. The snow was coming down harder, and there was enough on her silver Honda Fit already that she had to brush it off. Resolving not to complain, she gritted her teeth and did the chore, then hopped in quickly, glad the heat was already pouring out of the vents.

Loch Mallaig was hunkered down for the night, its businesses closed except for a restaurant or two. Some people still had their Christmas lights up, a cheery note in the otherwise almost total darkness.

When Molly reached the library, the small lot was full, as were the parking spaces in front. She drove slowly down the street looking for a spot, then grabbed the first one that was open. One benefit of having a compact car was that she could sneak in almost anywhere. She hopped out, grabbed her tote, and locked the car, then made her way down the sidewalk to the library, which was an attractive two-story brick building with tall windows.

Molly picked up her pace. She loved the library, the sense of history and learning and community it provided. She almost always had good conversations here, and she always found great new books to read.

As she approached the stone front steps, she saw a couple coming from the other direction. "Hello," she called. "Here for the meeting?"

"We sure are," the man answered.

As they drew closer, Molly realized it was Sheldon Barker and his wife, Sheila, who didn't look any happier than she had this afternoon out at the lake.

"I recognize you," Sheila said. "You were at that cottage today."

"I was," Molly said. "The other couple I was with will be here tonight too."

They climbed the steps, Molly and Sheila ahead of Sheldon. "Have you been a member of the historical society long?" he asked.

"I'm more of an auxiliary member, I guess you'd call it," Molly said as they entered the building. "I help out now and then, but I don't attend every meeting. The head of the society asked me and my friends to take part, especially because our bakehouse is supplying goods for some of the gatherings."

The library was warm and bright, a welcome respite from the cold night. As Molly slid out of her coat, she inhaled deeply, enjoying the mingled fragrances of paper, ink, wood, and furniture polish that characterized libraries. She'd loved them since she was a girl, when her family had made frequent trips to check out books.

"The meeting is upstairs," she told the Barkers, leading them to the wide marble staircase.

On the upper level, other people were already gathered in the conference room, including Fergus, who was talking to Mayor Tavish Calhoun, a retired dentist. Fergus noticed Molly and gave her a wave.

"Come with me," Molly said to Sheldon and Sheila. "I want you to meet some people." When she'd moved to town, others had done the honors, which had made her feel included and accepted.

When they reached Fergus and Tavish, Molly introduced the Barkers. Mayor Calhoun gave them a very warm welcome, his broad face beaming. "I'm so glad to meet you," he said. "And it's wonderful that you're already getting involved. Loch Mallaig needs more active citizens such as yourselves."

Sheila's face pinked, the sour expression lifting slightly. "We're very happy to be here." She gave her husband a cryptic glance. "It's always nice to get a fresh start. If you can leave the past behind."

What was that about? Molly wondered. Had the Barkers moved to town to escape something? It wasn't really her business, but she couldn't help being curious. Judging by Fergus's slightly lifted brows, he'd also noticed the innuendo.

Sheldon chuckled, his flushed cheeks the only sign of discomfort. Or were they still red from the cold? "We loved Marquette, but Sheila is right. It's exciting to enter a new phase of life." He pulled out a business card holder and gave both men a card. "I'm still running my insurance agency, so if you need coverage for anything, please give me a call. Quotes are free."

"Good evening, everyone," Grizela called. The full-figured, gray-haired librarian clapped her hands sharply. "It's time to get started."

The meeting attendees moved to a long table with a scrape of chairs. Molly hung her coat on a chair next to Fergus. While she was settling in, Carol, Harvey, and Laura bustled into the meeting room.

"Sorry we're late," Carol said. "We stopped to help someone who went off the road."

Molly was thankful she only had a couple of blocks to navigate to get home. Those who lived outside of the downtown area often had to deal with slippery roads.

Carol nodded at Sheila and Sheldon. "Nice to see you again," she murmured, putting her coat on the empty chairback beside Molly. She sat down, arranging her face in a bland expression in response to Grizela's frown of disapproval.

"All right, everyone." The librarian's shrewd green eyes surveyed the gathering. "We're ready to begin." She paused, dragging in a breath. "We have a problem. A very big problem. Our Robert Burns orator has had to back out. He's ill, but even if he hadn't been, his flight was canceled."

Despite the fact that all in attendance already knew this, a pall fell over the group. Everyone exchanged glances, seeming too tongue-tied to respond.

Brodie McCauley, owner of Neeps and Tatties, broke the silence. "This is bad for us, no doubt about it. We've already ordered the food for the dinner. Now what are we going to do with it all?"

"We have the same issue at the resort," Fergus said. "We're certainly not fully booked right now and were relying on the final Burns event being held at King's Heid Pub."

As the owner of a business that served food, Molly sympathized with the men's concerns. The difference was that the bakehouse didn't use a lot of perishable ingredients, so they'd eventually use up the extra Laura had ordered.

At the other end of the table, Vernon waved his hand.

"Yes, Vernon?" Grizela asked. She cracked a rare smile. "Are you volunteering to orate?"

"Och, no," Vernon protested with a scowl. "I came tonight because I have someone for ye. He's got the gift of gab all right. And he's a Burns scholar."

People along the table glanced around at each other again, but this time it was with interest and the faint dawning of hope.

"Who is this marvel?" Grizela asked. "And where is he?"

At the sound of feet on the marble stairs, Vernon gestured. "There he is now."

Molly wasn't overly surprised when Finlay Croft walked in. Harvey had said he was a professor. A woman with a long, dark braid was with him, her intense brown eyes peering from under the wool cap pulled low on her forehead. She had the weather-beaten complexion and assertive yet graceful movements of an athlete.

"Brrr," Finlay said with dramatic flair as he unwound his scarf. "A winter night not fit for man nor beast." He didn't seem to even notice that everyone was staring at him. He and his companion walked toward the only two open chairs at the table.

"Glad ye could come on short notice, Finlay," Vernon said. "These folks seem to be short an orator for the Burns Week." He glanced at Grizela, who nodded. "And we were wondering if you would consider stepping in."

Finlay's expression became thoughtful. "This coming week?" He pulled out a chair so his friend could sit, then lowered himself into his own seat. "I know a bit of Burns, if that's what you're asking." His cheeks puffed with pride as he glanced around the table. "I've been asked to recite a time or two."

The woman laughed, tossing her braid back. "More than once or twice. Finlay is practically on call when it comes to oration in our neck of the woods."

Grizela's lips pursed. "That is very good to hear. We'd be much obliged if you could perform for us, Finlay." She picked up two packets and handed them to Laura, who was sitting beside her. "Can you please pass this to Finlay and . . ." Her gray brows went up in inquiry.

"Jeanne Dupont," the woman said. "I own a cabin on the loch."

"I've seen you out fishing," Harvey said with a smile. "You've got quite a casting arm."

"Thank you." Jeanne tipped her chin in acknowledgment. "Loch Mallaig has become my home away from home."

Finlay cleared his throat, drawing attention back to himself. He'd been flipping through the pages, which detailed the event's venues, menus, and entertainment. In addition to orated poems, The Piping Yoopers and the Leaping Lowlanders would perform on multiple occasions.

"Nice little event you have here," Finlay said. "I'm impressed." He patted his chest. "Good thing I packed my best jacket. Although I will need a cravat for authenticity." He chuckled in his magnificent voice. "I didn't think to bring one."

"We can find something," Fergus promised. "Dressed to Kilt carries cravats, I believe."

"They do," Carol said. "I've seen them." She glanced at her husband, who shuddered and ran a hand over his face. Molly smiled, guessing Carol had tried to convince Harvey to wear one on some occasion or other.

Grizela relaxed in her seat, visibly relieved. "You've truly saved the day, Professor Croft. Well, actually you've saved the week. Now that's settled, let's do a run-through of the agenda. Does everyone have a packet?"

With a collective sigh of relief, the group turned their attention to the printed program and returned to the meeting's original plan. Once the discussion was finished, they broke for refreshments, which consisted of apple cider, hot tea, and decaf coffee, as well as a plate of Scottish shortbread and another platter with dark slices of a loaf-shaped cake.

"What's this?" Molly asked Grizela.

The librarian drew herself up with pride. "That is my own family's secret-recipe black bun. It uses raisins, currants, spices, and black treacle. It's usually a Hogmanay treat, but I always wish for it on a cold night such as this. I recommend it with a hot toddy on a particularly stormy evening. It is a very fortifying cake."

Molly eagerly sampled the treat, having tasted Grizela's other baked goods in the past. She'd been leery of its appearance, but the richly flavored cake did hit the spot. "This is wonderful," she enthused.

The older woman actually flushed a little. "*Wheesht*," she said modestly, though the word held none of its traditional harshness. Then again, Molly reflected, it was usually hissed at loud library visitors. "It's been passed down through generations, and each woman added her own touch to the recipe. Ronald always claims he decided to propose the first time he tasted my black bun." One of the other historical society members called for her, and the tenderness left her face, replaced by her customary sharpness as she moved to address the group nearby.

Wanting to warm up before heading back into the cold, Molly got in line for coffee. After dispensing a cup, she found herself waiting for Brodie McCauley to finish with the cream.

"I'm so glad we found an orator," Molly said to the restaurant owner. "That was a real last-minute save."

To her surprise, the usually cheerful Brodie remained stony faced as he finished doctoring his coffee. He glanced over to where Finlay was holding court, his voice easily carrying over the others in the room. "Sure I'm glad." With a sharp movement, he tossed the little red stirrer into the trash bucket. "But poor Uncle Jock would be rolling."

Molly added cream to her coffee and stirred as she stepped away from the table to make way for the next person in line. "About what happened at the fishing derby, you mean?"

Brodie gave her a puzzled frown over the rim of his cup. "What are you talking about?"

Molly sighed. She'd stepped into it now. Moving out of earshot of others, she said, "There was a little controversy at the weigh-in today." She nodded toward Finlay. "He's the judge."

Brodie's gaze rested on Finlay. "I'm not surprised. The man's ego is huge." His lips twisted in a grimace. "He and my uncle were good friends for years. Then he . . ." His voice trailed off and he shook his head. "Sorry, I shouldn't have brought it up. Please excuse me. I need to talk to my insurance agent."

"Of course," Molly said. "I take it you work with Sheldon?" He was the only insurance agent in the room. Brodie's wife, Catriona, was already speaking to the new resident.

"We do," Brodie said. "And unfortunately we have an insurance claim underway. Frozen pipes."

"Oh no," Molly said. "I'm so sorry to hear that." As a business owner, she was sensitive to the havoc that such problems could wreak on operations. "Will you be okay to host the opening dinner tomorrow night?"

"This was at home," Brodie said. "The pipes are fixed. We're waiting on the check from the company now. They've been a little slow processing our claim, but isn't that always the way?" He checked his watch. "I need to get going. Nice chatting with you, Molly."

As Molly watched him go, she felt both relieved and anxious. They had been fortunate to find a stand-in for their orator. But would Finlay Croft be more trouble than he was worth?

4

"Hurry," Laura called to Molly as they scurried toward Neeps and Tatties, shoulders hunched and chins tucked in their scarves against a fierce wind. The restaurant windows were bright against the gloomy night, beckoning like an oasis of warmth and cheer.

Molly reached the big wooden door first and held it open for her friend. Her cheeks felt scoured by the cold and wind, and she was sure they were beet red. "Whew," she said as they stepped into the steamy-warm building. "What a relief to get out of that cold."

The skirl of a bagpipe playing "Ye Banks and Braes" drifted from the main room, a sound that lifted Molly's heart.

"It's seriously raw out there," Laura said, shedding her coat and tucking gloves, hat, and scarf in the sleeves. She pushed aside other hanging coats to make room for hers and Molly's. "Today was even colder than yesterday."

Molly hung her coat next to Laura's. "I ought to freshen up before we go in," she said, sure she had a bad case of hat hair, one of winter's major problems.

The ladies' room was down a short hallway. Molly and Laura stood in front of the vanity to fix their hair and put on fresh lipstick.

"I like your outfit," Molly said as she shook her blonde bangs into place.

Laura was wearing a coppery silk blouse and cream-colored wool trousers with brown ankle boots on her feet. The colors set off her auburn hair and brown eyes nicely. "Thanks. You look great too."

A change from the casual, practical bakehouse outfits she usually wore, Molly had on a soft, pale blue sweater spangled with glittering beads across the bodice and charcoal-gray pants. "I bought this top the last time I went shopping in Houghton." That was another aspect of living in the beautiful and remote Upper Peninsula—real shopping required a long drive. "I finally had an occasion to wear it."

Laura tucked her lipstick into her bag, then gave herself one last glance in the mirror. "Ready?"

Molly peered at her own face, deciding that her pink cheeks were more flattering than not. "I'm ready."

At the hostess podium, Catriona McCauley greeted them. Petite with curly brown hair, the restaurant owner was wearing a full-sleeved blouse under a long plaid gown reminiscent of Scotland in the time of Robert Burns. "Good evening, ladies. Are you having the Burns buffet or our regular menu?"

"The buffet," Laura said, a hint of incredulity in her voice. "Are people really having regular food tonight?"

Catriona nodded. "We try to accommodate all tastes. A few of our customers aren't necessarily here for the Burns supper." Her gaze went to a group of men sitting in a booth, hunched over big plates of hamburgers and French fries.

Molly recognized the three fishermen from the contest who had argued with Finlay. Did they know he was the star attraction tonight? She wondered what they would think of that.

Laura and Molly followed Catriona through the restaurant toward a cluster of tables at the back. Fergus glanced up and waved as he saw them coming, making Molly's heart skip a beat. He patted the empty chair beside him. Carol and Harvey were already seated at the table, along with Hamish and his wife, Joyce.

"I figured you'd want to join this party," Catriona told Molly and

Laura. "Enjoy." She hurried away as a big group of people entered the restaurant.

After exchanging greetings, Molly settled into the chair Fergus had saved for her between him and Carol, who had Harvey on her other side.

"This is nice," Molly said, admiring the atmosphere. Candles flickered on the tables, which were covered with plaid tablecloths and decorated with low arrangements of white roses and heather. A short distance away, a fire roared in the huge fireplace, adding to the cozy ambience.

Fergus sighed. "It certainly is. A respite from the cold and the bustle of daily life." He lifted a jug. "Sparkling cider?"

"Please," Molly said, removing her white linen napkin from its ring and placing it on her lap. She glanced around the restaurant.

The bagpiper, whom Molly now recognized as The Piping Yoopers leader Alastair Thomson, segued into "Flow Gently, Sweet Afton," a Burns poem that had been set to music in the 19th century. A long table against the wall held chafing dishes. Servers, including Noah Taggart, bustled about, adding food from wheeled carts to the buffet. Delicious aromas drifted their way, and Molly was suddenly ravenous.

Fergus leaned closer. "Are you going to try the haggis tonight?" His smile was teasing.

Molly swallowed, thinking about the McCauleys' recipe—a mixture of ground lamb, oatmeal, onions, beef liver, and spices cooked inside a sheep's stomach. "I think so. I mean, it's only fitting at a Burns supper, right?" She liked all the ingredients separately, so it couldn't be that bad. Fortunately they weren't serving the original Scottish version, which included additional ingredients that definitely gave Molly pause.

"You'll enjoy it," Hamish said. "Even if it is a poor imitation. Joyce and I go for the authentic fare when we visit Scotland."

"Hamish insists," Joyce said, rolling her brown eyes and grinning. "And you know he always gets his way." Plump and rosy-cheeked with a sunny personality, Joyce was unperturbed by Hamish's frequent grumps.

"Away with ye, woman," Hamish said. "It's the other way 'round, I think."

In response, his wife smiled and batted her eyelashes at him. Even after forty-five years of marriage, they were obviously in love.

Grizela and a few other members of the society entered, one man carrying an easel under his arm. At Grizela's direction, he set up the easel, and another volunteer placed something covered on it.

"I wonder what that is," Carol said to Molly. "Maybe a painting."

"I imagine we'll find out soon enough," Molly said, curious herself. She sipped cider and relaxed, watching the other seats fill up. Sheldon and Sheila Barker arrived and sat with Finlay and Jeanne. Finlay was decked out in a black velvet coat with white cravat, his hair oiled down into an approximation of a Robert Burns style.

The three fishermen were sitting in her line of sight, and she witnessed their reaction to Finlay, the nudges, whispers, and chuckles. Hopefully they wouldn't heckle Finlay's performance.

Instead of sitting at her place, Grizela remained standing and tapped a knife on a glass. The murmur of conversation died down, and even the servers began to move more quietly.

"Good evening, everyone," the librarian said. As suited her role as chair, she was bedecked in traditional plaid, sash, and blouse. "I'm thrilled to see such a good turnout for the kickoff of Loch Mallaig's Burns Week. Welcome."

The audience clapped and she nodded acknowledgment.

"We've got a wonderful dinner ahead of us." Grizela gestured at the laden buffet table. "The haggis will be piped in shortly, as befits a proper Burns supper. But before we eat, I'd like to tell you a little about this poet who is truly the voice of our homeland, Scotland."

One of the fishermen cackled at this flowery description, the sound swiftly cut off when a friend shushed him.

Grizela cocked a brow in their direction, then nodded to the volunteer who had carried the easel. He whipped off the cloth to reveal a portrait of a man—or at least that's what it seemed to be.

Molly thought it was supposed to depict Robert Burns, but the painting was rather abstract so she couldn't be sure. Although abstract art wasn't her preference, she could tell that the artist who had painted it was talented. But over at the fishermen's table, no such appreciation for art was shown. All three of them roared with laughter.

Grizela shot them the ferocious scowl she usually reserved for especially boisterous library patrons and made a chopping motion. The men got the message and subsided, only occasional snickers escaping.

"This striking portrait," Grizela said, "was painted by a new member of the historical society." Her gaze searched the room and found Sheila Barker. She motioned for the woman to stand. "Sheila Barker is generously allowing us to exhibit the painting all week, and at the conclusion of our festivities, a lucky attendee will take Robert Burns home." Grizela applauded, and others joined in. "Thank you, Sheila."

The artist bowed, face flaming from the fishermen's reaction, and plopped back into her seat. Finlay whispered something to Jeanne, who frowned and shot Sheila a sympathetic look.

Once the applause died, Grizela pulled out a sheaf of notes and proceeded to give an overview of Robert Burns's life. The man now regarded as Scotland's national bard had seen very little financial success during his short life of thirty-seven years. His attempts at farming and various trades failed, but he managed to write volumes of poetry, collect traditional folk songs, and pen more than three hundred songs of his own. He also fathered twelve children and had numerous descendants. And his work influenced many who came after him, including poets William Wordsworth, Samuel Taylor Coleridge, and Percy Bysshe Shelley.

Hamish appeared thoughtful as Grizela wrapped up her oral history. "I wonder if I might be related to Burns," he said. He often claimed to be a descendant of Robert the Bruce, another famous figure in Scottish history.

His wife grinned as she patted his arm. "Maybe so. You've certainly got the gift of gab."

Grizela put away her notes. "And now, ladies and gentlemen," she said, nodding to Alastair. "In line with the great tradition inspired by Burns's poem 'Address to a Haggis,' it's time to pipe in our main dish."

Alastair, who was already standing near a swinging door to the kitchen, struck up a tune. The door opened and Noah Taggart emerged, lugging a silver tray holding a huge haggis, which looked like a giant sausage.

The three fishermen were beside themselves at the sight, laughing and pointing. Fortunately, the bagpipes drowned out their comments.

Alastair led Noah to the serving table, where the younger man lowered the tray to a place of prominence. Another server, wielding a long silver knife, sliced into it with a flourish. Everyone cheered.

Finlay stood, smoothing his jacket into place, and went to stand by the table. His deep voice boomed out as he recited a few verses of the poem that had inspired the presentation of the haggis. He followed that up with a recitation of "Selkirk Grace," another Burns supper tradition. After everyone murmured "Amen," more cheering erupted as Finlay bowed and returned to his seat.

"We'll hear more from our bard during dessert," Grizela said. "Now, it's time to eat. Line up, everyone, and enjoy."

The guests approached the buffet in groups by table. Molly was absolutely starving by the time it was her turn, but she warned herself to take it easy. The temptation to load her plate was too great when there were so many choices.

In addition to a small helping of haggis, servings of potatoes and turnips—neeps and tatties—were required, as was a bowl of cullen skink, a creamy smoked fish soup. Molly took some green vegetables for variety and a sausage roll in case she didn't like the haggis.

Catriona was circulating through the tables, bringing baskets of bread and drinks that people were ordering. "Coffee or tea?" she asked Molly's table once they were all seated again. "We're bringing out hot drinks with dessert."

"I'll take decaf coffee, please," Molly said. She took a tentative bite of the haggis. Crumbly and spicy, it reminded her of regular pork sausage. *Really, if you don't think about the casing or the Scottish version, it's totally fine.*

Fergus nudged her. "What do you think?"

"Not bad," Molly said. She scooped up a mouthful of buttery neeps and tatties. "But these are my favorites. They're the perfect comfort food for a cold night." The soup was good too, rich and savory.

From a nearby table, Finlay snapped his fingers in the air. "Miss? Miss!" he called. Jeanne scowled and put a restraining hand on his arm, but the professor pulled away and continued snapping.

Catriona, who had been standing with her back to Finlay, whirled around at the summons. Molly saw a frown crease her brow, but then it was as though something had wiped her expression clean. "How can I help you?" she asked the professor, her tone polite.

Molly couldn't hear what he said, but she noticed Finlay pointing at his food, obviously lodging a complaint. Catriona picked up his plate and waved Noah over. They conferred, then Noah went to the buffet and made up a new plate with a different selection of food.

Molly wondered if Finlay's star status had gone to his head or if he was always so rude. He accepted the plate from Noah with only a scant nod, then proceeded to examine its contents. Noah rushed away, his head down.

As dinner came to a close, the guests began to get up and mill about. Over at the buffet table, the food was being cleared away in preparation for dessert. Finlay stood in a corner, glancing over notes and mumbling to himself.

"I'm off to the ladies' room," Laura said, putting her napkin on the table and rising.

Carol pushed back her chair. "Me too." She nudged Harvey. "Don't start dessert without me."

He winked in reply, then went back to discussing fly fishing with Fergus and Hamish. Joyce went along as well, but Molly stayed.

As Laura walked by the fishermen's table, one of them said something to her. She stopped to talk, waving Carol and Joyce on. Laura was single and often dated, but Molly sincerely doubted these burly, coarse men were her type. When her friend began to point a finger as if giving directions, she realized Laura was probably just answering an inquiry. A minute later, she gave them a friendly smile, said something that made them laugh, and continued on to the restroom.

Dessert choices included shortbread and assorted biscuits from Bread on Arrival, toffee pudding, and cranachan, a confection of whipped cream, raspberries, and oats. Molly took a little of both puddings, gratified to see that the cookies were disappearing fast. Back at the table with her treats and piping hot coffee in front of her, Molly settled in to listen to Finlay's performance.

And what a performance it was. He read about half a dozen poems, including "A Red, Red Rose," "A Mother's Lament for the Death of Her Son," and more. His emotive voice and perfect inflection carried the entire audience to Scotland's heather-covered hills and snowy peaks, its rippling streams and deep, still lochs. The crowd was spellbound and, at the end, the applause was fervent.

Grizela stood once Finlay had returned to his seat. "Wasn't that wonderful? And to think that Professor Croft wasn't our planned speaker, since our original orator was unable to come. But the professor kindly stepped in and we thank him."

Finlay inclined his head in acknowledgment of more clapping.

"This Burns supper is only the beginning of our weeklong celebration," Grizela went on. "We have upcoming performances by The Leaping Lowlanders and The Piping Yoopers. Also, there will be a student poetry slam at Superior Bay College featuring work inspired by Robert Burns."

After a few more housekeeping notes, Grizela wrapped up her speech and the crowd began to thin out. Molly wasn't quite ready to leave, however. Catriona had refilled her coffee cup, and the steaming decaf offered a warm refuge from the cold night.

"Are you ready for more fishing tomorrow?" Fergus asked Harvey.

"I'm always ready for more fishing," Harvey said. "Are you planning to throw in a line?"

"I'll try to pop over for a while." Fergus grinned. "I have a good excuse. The resort is one of the sponsors."

Finlay approached the table, and Molly noticed that Jeanne had already left, as had the Barkers. Hamish and Joyce were also gone, and the professor leaned on the back of a vacated chair. "Good evening," he said. "Did I hear a mention of the fishing tournament?"

Harvey nodded, though the motion was reserved. "Yes, we're both going tomorrow."

Without invitation, Finlay pulled out the chair and sat. "You both seem like reasonable gentlemen," he said without preamble. "What did you think of that fracas yesterday afternoon?" He folded his arms. "That fish was a ringer. I don't care what Vernon said."

Molly glanced over at the table where the fishermen had been sitting and noticed to her relief that they were gone. According to someone Molly had overheard, Vernon hadn't attended the dinner because he'd suddenly come down with a head cold.

Fergus cleared his throat. "Actually, I've seen fish of that size come out of the loch. I wouldn't be too hasty to accuse people of cheating. It's all in good fun anyway, and for a good cause."

"That's right," Harvey said. "The derby benefits our town recreation program for children, which includes fishing lessons."

Finlay's brows rose. "I hope the telling of tall tales is discouraged by their instructors. Although I understand fish stories are de rigueur among sportsmen."

At the professor's patronizing tone, Harvey's face reddened and he leaned across the table. "Not in my circle. We pride ourselves on our honesty here in Loch Mallaig."

Fergus put out a hand. "It's okay, Harvey." He turned to Finlay, his blue eyes steely. "Perhaps you should consider stepping down, Finlay, if you can't enter into the spirit of our event."

With a grunt, Finlay pushed back the chair and stood. "Perhaps I should. After all, I'm pretty busy saving your little . . . whatever you call this haphazard to-do." He gazed around with clear derision. "I suppose this is as close to a celebratory event for a great poet as this town can manage. Good night." He pivoted on his heel and strode toward the restaurant exit, head high.

A brief silence fell over the table. "I'm sorry," Carol said. "You know I hate to speak ill of anyone, but that man is insufferable."

Fergus gave a little laugh. "I'm afraid I agree. I'll give Vernon a call first thing in the morning."

Harvey's brows knit. "Sounds like we need to find another judge. I suppose I can step in."

"But you're already in the tournament," Fergus said. "I'll do it. Castleglen is sponsoring the tournament, after all."

Catriona had circled back to their table, coffee carafe in hand. "Would anyone like a refill?"

Before they could answer, her husband dashed up to the table. "I'll be right back, Cat." He waved his phone. "The temperature monitor took a dip."

She groaned. "The furnace is acting up again?"

He nodded. "Seems so. I'll see if I can get it started. If not, I'll put in an emergency call." He hurried off.

Catriona shook her head. "We've had so much trouble this winter. After our furnace quit and some pipes froze, Brodie bought a monitoring system."

"That's wise," Fergus said. "We have sensors all over the resort. Sometimes guests leave their balcony doors wide open in winter, believe it or not." He turned to Molly. "I'm ready to head out. How about you?"

Laura and Carol wanted to stay a few more minutes, so Fergus offered to walk Molly home to the bakery across the street. He courteously helped her on with her coat, and together they stepped out into the cold parking lot.

"Be careful," he said. "It's icy out here."

She slid her hand into the crook of his elbow, and he guided her across the slippery pavement.

As they skirted a large truck, a dreadful sight brought them to a halt. In the feeble light of a streetlamp, Finlay Croft lay faceup on the ground, arms flung wide. A long, thin rod protruded from his chest.

5

Molly inhaled sharply, the frigid air burning her lungs. "Finlay," she croaked.

Before she could move, Fergus bounded over to the lifeless man and hunkered down, pressing his fingers to Finlay's neck. Her heart plummeted when he shook his head.

"He's dead," Fergus said.

His grim statement made Molly shiver. She glanced around the shadowed parking lot, suddenly aware that Finlay's killer might be lurking nearby. She felt terribly exposed and vulnerable.

Fergus stood and fished around in his pocket. "You should go back inside, Molly," he said as he removed his phone. "It's freezing out here." The phone screen lit his face as he tapped at it. "I'm calling the police."

To Molly's surprise, she was reluctant to leave despite the potential danger, feeling as though she and Fergus should stay near Finlay until help arrived. "I'm not going anywhere," she said. "Not until the police come. Plus I'm a witness since we were first on the scene."

Fergus nodded in acknowledgment, then began to speak into the phone. While waiting, Molly moved closer to a large SUV that blocked the cold wind and bounced up and down on her toes, trying to stay warm. When a man came striding across the parking lot, she flinched, shrinking back into the shadows.

But as he drew closer, she recognized Brodie, who must have been on his way to the back entrance of the restaurant. When he saw Fergus, he halted, then changed course and trotted over. "What's going on? Is someone hurt?"

Fergus disconnected. "Finlay is dead. The police are on their way."

Brodie stood at a short distance, staring down at the stricken professor with horror. "What happened?" He bent closer. "Is that my—" He broke off abruptly.

"I thought you went home," Molly said.

"I did," Brodie replied, still staring down at Finlay. "I live a couple of blocks away. It's quicker and easier to walk, especially since my truck is blocked in."

Whirling emergency lights cut through the gloom, and two Loch Mallaig cruisers pulled into the parking lot, followed by an ambulance.

Police Chief Owen Thomson emerged from the first cruiser and made his way toward them. "What do we have here?"

Molly immediately felt better at the sight of the tall, capable chief with his authoritative demeanor. If anyone could get this horrifying situation to make sense, it was Chief Thomson.

Fergus gestured toward the body. "I was walking Molly home when we saw Finlay lying on the ground. He also attended tonight's event."

The chief hunkered down to check Finlay's vitals. "How long ago was that? And how long had it been since you'd seen him?"

Fergus checked the time on his phone. "We've been out here almost ten minutes, but I haven't been paying attention to the time this evening. Molly, do you remember when he left the restaurant?"

She nodded. "About half an hour ago. Some of the other people at my table can probably confirm that." With a start, Molly realized that Carol and Laura had no idea what had happened.

Chief Thomson glanced around at the vehicles in the lot, then spoke to two other officers who had joined them. "Head inside and tell everyone to stay put for the moment. We'll want to talk to them before they leave." He turned to Molly, who was no longer able to repress a shiver. "Go get warmed up inside, but please don't talk to anyone." He shifted his focus to Brodie. "And you, Mr. McCauley. When did you arrive on the scene?"

As Molly walked toward the restaurant door, she heard Brodie explaining that he'd just been to his house. And no, he hadn't seen Finlay lying there when he'd gone home.

But he'd left the restaurant after Finlay, Molly remembered. Finlay must have been somewhere in the parking lot when Brodie came out. With a jolt, she realized that if Finlay had already been dead, Brodie might not have seen him in the dark.

Deputy Chief Broderick Gillespie held the door open for Molly to enter. "How are you doing?" he asked, his hazel eyes creased with concern. Gillespie was tall, with the black hair and light brown skin of his Chippewa mother. Like the rest of the small force, he was a good officer, well-liked by the community he served so faithfully.

"I'm okay," Molly answered, shivering again. Was it the cold or shock setting in? Perhaps it was the sight of Oliver Fitzgerald, the coroner and local funeral home director, pulling up to the scene. "I'm only a little shaken up."

"No wonder," the deputy chief said, following her into the building with a younger officer, Dalziel Murdoch, coming in behind them. Inside the restaurant, Gillespie gestured to Catriona, who came bustling over, wiping her hands on her apron.

"Is everything all right?" Catriona asked, glancing between the officers and Molly.

Across the room, Molly saw Laura and Carol watching her with concern. Laura jumped to her feet, but Molly shook her head and gestured for her to stay put.

Gillespie lowered his voice. "A man was found dead outside. We'll need to question everyone here."

Catriona gasped, a hand flying to her mouth. "Not Brodie?" She looked to Molly. "Or Fergus?"

"They're both fine," Molly said quickly.

"It's Finlay Croft," Gillespie said. "Could you help with a few things, Mrs. McCauley? I need a place to interview people, and a warm seat and a hot drink for Mrs. Ferris. She's had a bit of a shock."

"Of course." His requests seemed to snap Catriona out of a fog of confusion. "You can use the office, such as it is, to talk to people. And Molly, come with me. I'll get you a hot chocolate."

Gillespie dispatched the other officer to talk to Molly's friends and the rest of the guests and staff. Molly wished she could talk to her friends now, but she knew they'd catch up later. Catriona settled her in a seat right next to the huge fireplace, where a small yet warm fire flickered.

From this vantage point, sipping on hot chocolate, she watched as the officers efficiently organized a process to speak to people before releasing them to go home. Once in a while, she forced a brave smile when Carol and Laura glanced her way.

One by one, guests and staff went into the office to talk to Gillespie and then were released. Every time Molly heard the front door open and shut, she wished she was among them. Now warmer and needing to stretch her legs, she got up and wandered around the almost empty restaurant. Peeking through a window with a view of the parking lot, Molly saw that bright lights had been set up to illuminate the scene. Figures moved about, doing their grim jobs.

The restaurant door opened, and a shivering Fergus stepped inside. "It's brutal out there," he said, stamping his feet on the rug. He threw Molly a smile, then moved to the fireplace to warm up.

Molly longed to talk to Fergus, to rehash the horrific experience they had shared, but she knew better. Once they had been interviewed, they could talk. But right now it was essential that recollections of the evening remain untainted by someone else's impressions.

Officer Murdoch approached Molly. "Mrs. Ferris? Please come with me."

Her palms grew clammy. She had been questioned by the police before, but it never got easier. As she followed the slender, blond officer across the carpet, she glanced at Fergus. He gave her a reassuring nod.

Chief Thomson was in the small office, along with the deputy chief. Thomson's presence meant that Molly was a key witness, a realization that made her heart pound. Whatever she said—or didn't say—might have a huge bearing on the direction of the case.

"Have a seat," the chief said, his voice kind. "Are you feeling a little better?"

She nodded as she settled into the chair. "Warmer, anyway. Well enough to help however I can."

"I appreciate that. First I'd like to ask you about the discovery of the body. And then we'll talk about the events of this evening."

"Okay," Molly said, her mouth dry. She clasped her hands together. "Go ahead."

While Gillespie took notes, Molly explained how Fergus had offered to walk her home across the street. When she got to the part where they spotted Finlay, the picture was so clear in her mind that she couldn't repress a shudder. "At first I thought he might have fallen and hit his head—it's pretty icy out there—or that he was ill. But then we saw that rod sticking out of his chest."

"It was an arrow," Thomson said. "The fletching—the feathers on the end—is quite small."

"That's like the Burns poem," Molly blurted. "Finlay recited it tonight." She did a quick search on her phone. "Here it is. 'A Mother's Lament for the Death of Her Son.' It's very sad. 'Fate gave the word, the arrow sped, And pierc'd my darling's heart.'"

The policemen exchanged glances, and Molly wondered what they were thinking. Perhaps that she was seeing connections where they didn't exist.

"Anyway," she said with a shrug of one shoulder. "It's an odd coincidence."

Gillespie made a note as Thomson asked, "Did Finlay Croft attend the dinner alone tonight?"

Molly wondered if he already knew the answer and was double-checking. "I think he was with Jeanne Dupont, but she left before he did. She's also a professor at the college where Finlay teaches. Taught, I mean." She wondered if Jeanne and Finlay were dating, although she hadn't seen any overt signs of affection between the pair.

"Any conflicts between Finlay and other guests?" Thomson asked.

Molly reviewed the evening in her mind, cringing at the thought of implicating anyone. "Well, he was rude to Catriona when she was waiting on tables. But that seems rather minor." She remembered the fishermen. "There were three men here who had argued with Finlay at the fishing tournament. A lot of people witnessed that argument, including Harvey and Carol MacCallan and Noah Taggart, who was also serving here tonight." Where was Noah? She hadn't seen him leave, but that didn't mean anything. He might have used the rear entrance.

"We'll follow up on that." Thomson paused. "Vernon Pennycook didn't attend tonight, did he?"

"No. I heard he was sick with a cold," Molly said. "He's the one who suggested Finlay orate the Burns poetry for us. Our original orator canceled due to illness and the weather." Did they really suspect Vernon or were they simply being thorough? Had Vernon lured Finlay here tonight with the offer of a star appearance and then shot him with an arrow?

Molly's head spun. She was obviously overtired, and now her thoughts were bordering on the ridiculous.

Thomson asked Molly to list any other guests who had left before Finlay, and she did her best. "Grizela might be able to help," she said. "I'm sure she paid attention to who attended. And Catriona too. She was waiting on everyone."

The chief nodded. "What about staff? Any idea when they left?"

"No," Molly said. "Not really. Except Brodie. He said he had to run home for a minute to check the heat. That was right after Finlay left."

Once again, the officers exchanged glances. Molly recalled what Brodie had blurted. "Is that my—" Arrow? He'd seemed surprised to see it, which he wouldn't be if he had been the one to launch it, right?

Molly rubbed her temples, the tired feeling in her head building into an ache. She had to tell them what she'd heard. Fergus had heard it too, but he might have forgotten.

"I think Brodie might have recognized the arrow," she said. "Or thought it was one like his." She quoted him exactly, doing her best to imitate his inflection.

Chief Thomson rose to standing. "Thank you, Molly. We appreciate your candor. You can go home now, but please, if you think of any other details from tonight, give me a call."

Molly said good night and wandered back out to the main room. Fergus was already on his way into the office, but he paused. "Molly, if you can wait a little longer, I'll walk you home."

"Thanks, Fergus," she said, heading over to the comfort of the fire. "I'll wait."

Dishes clattered in the kitchen, and Molly guessed Catriona and Brodie were still cleaning up from the meal. She wished she had something to do besides sit and brood about what had happened. Who had killed Finlay? And why?

Molly jumped up and began to pace the empty restaurant, certain that she would have the carpet memorized before Fergus returned.

Finally she heard the office door open. Fergus walked into the dining room, his gaze seeking her. "Ready?" he asked. His face was drawn, and he was clearly exhausted, she noticed with sympathy.

"Very," she replied.

As Molly was slipping her coat on, she heard raised voices in the kitchen. Then the swinging doors burst open and Chief Thomson and Deputy Chief Gillespie emerged, holding the arms of a figure between them.

It was Brodie McCauley. And he was wearing handcuffs.

6

Catriona bolted out of the kitchen, her pretty features twisted in distress. "You can't arrest him," she cried. "He's innocent!"

But the police officers didn't respond as they continued to shepherd Brodie toward the door. Brodie glanced back over his shoulder at his wife. "It will be all right, Cat. Call a lawyer."

After the front door swung shut behind the men, Catriona burst into tears. "I can't believe this is happening. Brodie didn't kill anyone." She found a tissue in her apron and mopped at her eyes.

Fergus glanced at Molly then went to Catriona's side. "And we believe you." He put an arm around her and guided her toward a chair near the fire.

Molly dashed ahead and added another log. Using a poker, she prodded the almost dormant flames into new life.

"I don't even know where to begin," Catriona said, twisting her hands. "Where do I find a lawyer? The only ones I know handle real estate and wills."

Fergus rubbed his chin, thoughtful. "I can make a few calls for you, if you like."

"Would you?" The firelight flickered in Catriona's eyes, which were wet with tears. "I'd really appreciate it."

"Of course," he said.

The chef swallowed visibly. "I feel like I've stepped into a nightmare. I should have known. Everything has been going so well. Almost too well." Her laugh was bitter. "Now what's going to happen to us?" She waved a hand at the restaurant. "We gave up everything to move here from Chicago and take over this place after Brodie's uncle died. He loved his job as a fireman, you know. But I was excited about this opportunity to run my own restaurant. Cooking under another chef was all pressure, no glory."

Molly had been only dimly aware of the couple's background. She imagined their exciting and busy life in the city, both of them with careers on the rise. But, as it had for Molly herself and so many others, Loch Mallaig promised a richer, more relaxing life.

"Now what are we going to do?" Catriona's hands tightened in the apron. "Everything is ruined." A note of panic came into her voice as it rose.

"We're going to take one step at a time," Molly said in the most soothing voice she could muster. "Fergus will call attorneys and we'll find the best, someone who will get the charges dropped."

Fergus had been staring into the fire, his gaze distant. Now he shifted in his chair. "Catriona, a main piece of evidence is that one of Brodie's arrows could have been used. Where did he keep them?"

Molly held her breath, waiting for the answer. This was a very important question. If they had been at home, that implicated Brodie even further since he said he'd gone there this evening. But maybe someone had stolen the bow and arrows, either when visiting or while Brodie and Catriona were at work.

"As far as I know," Catriona said, "they were here, in the office closet. He put them there after target practice a couple of days ago. He goes to the indoor range."

"Do you keep the office locked?" Fergus asked.

She pressed her lips together and shook her head. "No, not usually. We secure the cash and our checkbooks. But we're always in and out of the office for one thing or another."

Fergus locked eyes with Molly, and she could guess what he was thinking. Anyone—a guest or one of the staff—could have grabbed the bow and arrows tonight.

"I think that information certainly broadens the field of suspects," Fergus said. "Anyone could have gone out the back door after swiping the bow and arrows."

Hope dawned on Catriona's face. "They sure could. People go out that door all the time. You can't get in that way without a key, though."

Molly tapped her chin thoughtfully. "But someone might have left the door propped open a bit so as to slip in and out."

Fergus nodded. "Very good point, Molly. These are all issues to raise with the attorney."

Catriona slumped tiredly. "I hope I can remember them all. Right now my brain feels like mush."

"You've had a huge shock," Molly said sympathetically. On impulse, she added, "And you're coming home with me. I don't want you to be alone tonight."

"Oh thank you, Molly." The chef offered a small, tired smile of appreciation. "I was dreading going home. The house will feel so empty without Brodie." Her hands twisted again. "Of course I won't get a wink of sleep. Not while my husband is in jail."

"I'm sure the attorney will ask for bail," Fergus said. "Let me walk you two to Molly's, then I'll make some calls."

"It's almost eleven. Will attorneys take calls so late?" Molly asked.

Fergus shrugged. "Maybe. I can leave messages too. I'm sure criminal attorneys are used to late-night calls."

Molly nodded grimly, then placed a hand on Catriona's arm. "Are you ready to go?"

Catriona stood and untied her apron strings. "I need to switch off some lights, lock up, and get my bag. Oh, and if you don't mind, can we swing by the house for a minute? I want to grab a toothbrush and a change of clothes."

"Of course," Fergus said. "I'll drive you over. I can start calling people while you lock up here."

Molly listened as Fergus left a few messages, but he never connected with a live person. Within five minutes, Catriona was ready to go, and they stepped out into the night. While Catriona was locking the door, Molly tried to avert her gaze from the crime scene, empty now of officers. The ambulance had gone, transporting Finlay's body to the morgue.

A cruiser pulled into the lot.

"Now what?" Catriona demanded as she pocketed her keys.

Deputy Chief Gillespie got out of the vehicle. "Mrs. McCauley?" he said. "We have search warrants for the restaurant and your home." He handed her a piece of paper.

The department certainly wasn't wasting any time. It was understandable—important evidence might begin to disappear the longer they waited. Although in this case, there shouldn't be any evidence since Brodie was innocent.

"Search warrants?" Catriona huffed in dismay as she took the papers, using the outside light mounted near the door to scan them. Then she handed her key ring to the deputy chief. "These are the restaurant keys. Please lock up when you're done."

"Does this mean we can't go inside Catriona's house?" Molly asked Gillespie. "We were going to swing by and pick up clothing and personal items. She's spending the night with me."

He considered the situation. "I'll have Officer Anderson meet you. She can accompany you inside while you gather your things."

Catriona sighed. "Right away, I hope. I'm bushed. And I live on Highland Street, not very far."

"I'm on it," Gillespie promised. He spoke into his chest mic. "She'll meet you there in five," he informed them a few moments later.

Fergus led the way to his Range Rover, pressing the key fob to unlock the doors. Molly let Catriona have the front passenger seat so she could guide Fergus to her home. He started the car and let it warm for a minute, then drove slowly out of the lot, using the entrance opposite to where the cruiser sat. After a few minutes, they arrived at the McCauley home, an attractive two-story cottage with lacy trim.

"This was Brodie's uncle's house," Catriona said. "We were lucky to buy it along with the restaurant."

A cruiser pulled up in front and Officer Greer Anderson got out. Molly was relieved the young woman had been assigned. She was kind as well as competent, and Molly was extra glad to see her.

"Will you come in with me, Molly?" Catriona asked. Her voice shook with nerves.

Molly reached for the door handle. "If it's okay with Greer."

The officer was waiting for them on the front walk. After greeting them, she said, "We'll need to be quick. Chief's orders."

"No problem," Catriona said. "I only need to grab a few things from my bedroom and bathroom." She moved briskly up the pavement to the front porch, where she fumbled in her pocket for the key.

"You'll have to stay in the front hall, Molly," Officer Anderson said.

"That's fine." Molly stood aside as Catriona twisted the key and used a gloved hand to open the door. At Greer's gesture, Molly followed Catriona inside, the officer taking up the rear.

Even though it was dimly lit, Molly quickly saw how gracious and charming the house was, with its tasteful wallpaper and gleaming hardwood floors. Straight ahead was a staircase, and open archways to each side provided glimpses of a living room and a dining room.

But what really caught her eye was the compound bow and quiver of arrows lying on the entrance hall floor.

Catriona gasped. "How did those get here?" She started forward.

"Stop, Mrs. McCauley," Officer Anderson barked. "Those are evidence. You can't touch them."

Catriona froze and stared wide-eyed at the officer.

"You can go upstairs," Greer said in a gentler tone, "but that's all. Hang on a second." Stepping aside, she spoke into her radio. Then she ushered Catriona up the stairs, leaving Molly standing in the hall. She turned back. "Don't touch a thing, Molly. You understand?"

"I do," Molly said, noting Greer's commanding tone. Someone had placed the bow and arrows in the house, although Catriona had said they had been in the restaurant office.

Had Brodie dumped them here after killing Finlay? It certainly appeared that way. Rebellion rose in Molly. She couldn't believe Brodie was guilty. Someone must have tried to frame him, and they were doing a really good job.

Molly glanced around the hallway. How had someone gotten in? She didn't see any sign of a security system, which wasn't unusual in Loch Mallaig. Crime was low in this little town, with very few break-ins or thefts.

Footsteps sounded in the upstairs hallway, and soon Catriona and Officer Anderson appeared at the top of the stairs. Catriona carried a small overnight bag. As the restaurant owner descended the steps, her expression was haunted, her shock evident in the stiff way she held her shoulders. Not glancing toward the incriminating bow and arrows, she said to Molly, "Are you ready to get out of here?"

"I certainly am." Molly opened the door for her. They hurried to the Range Rover and climbed inside.

"That didn't take long," Fergus said, putting the vehicle into gear.

A dense silence fell, then Catriona said, "Brodie's bow and arrows were in the front hall. I have no idea how they got there."

"Sounds like someone is definitely trying to frame your husband," Fergus murmured.

"Who would do such a thing?" Catriona exclaimed. "It's bad enough that a man was killed right in front of our restaurant, but to point the finger at Brodie? That's evil."

Fergus cast a concerned glance at her. "You're right, it is. I know it's hard, but try not to think too far ahead. Donal McNab, the best attorney in this area, called me back and agreed to talk to you in the morning, as early as you want. That's the first step."

Catriona's laugh sounded like cracking glass. "Oh, it will be early. There's no way I'll get any sleep tonight."

Within moments, Fergus was parking in the bakehouse driveway. He opened his door.

"You don't have to come up," Molly said.

"I'll sleep better if I know you both are safe," he said, sliding out. He first opened Molly's door, then went around to help Catriona out.

The trio went up the outside steps to Molly's door, which she unlocked. Angus barked inside, then whined, having recognized his owner's presence. While Angus scurried out to greet her, Molly let Catriona and Fergus enter first. She waited a minute while Angus did his rounds in the yard, then he bounded back up the steps and she ushered him back inside.

"I'll let you two get some rest," Fergus said once Molly had returned. "But promise you'll call me if anything happens, okay?"

Molly nodded, hoping that nothing would disturb them tonight. "See you tomorrow?"

"I'll come to the bakehouse bright and early." He brought out his phone and tapped the screen a few times. "Catriona, I've texted you Donal's contact information."

"Thanks so much, Fergus," she said. "I assume he has a good reputation, or you wouldn't have recommended him."

Fergus smiled. "I'll put it this way—his nickname is Bulldog, and it has nothing to do with his looks. He was named one of the best criminal attorneys in Michigan a couple of years ago."

Molly had heard of Donal McNab and was glad that he would take the case. "Good job, Fergus. Brodie is going to have excellent representation."

"He deserves it," Fergus said simply. "I'll bid you both good night." Angus yipped at his feet and Fergus laughed before bending to pat him. "I mean, bid you *three* good night." Angus licked his hand, pleased to be recognized.

After Fergus left, Angus shifted his attention to winning over a new friend, Catriona, while Molly put on the kettle. "I have some soothing herbal blends," she said to her guest. "Or I can make regular tea."

Catriona, who was now sitting with Angus in her lap, said, "Soothing, please. I need all the help I can get."

"Me too," Molly admitted. She was beyond tired but still reeling with shock from their discovery of the bow and arrows. She would have expected the killer to dispose of them somewhere else. It was almost as if the killer had overplayed his or her hand. Who would believe that Brodie had left his equipment right where the police would find it? Of course, one might argue that Brodie wasn't in his right mind, that he'd shot Finlay on impulse and then discarded the weapon in a panic.

The shriek of the teakettle interrupted Molly's thoughts, which were growing ever more tangled. It wasn't her job to sort all this out, she told herself firmly as she picked up the kettle. Let the police and Donal "Bulldog" McNab do it.

Molly poured boiling water in the waiting mugs, then brought them to the table along with honey and milk. She also found a container of soft lemon cookies and set them out. She gave Angus a treat, and, still seated on Catriona's lap, he gobbled it up.

Catriona smiled at the dog's antics, her hand gentle as she smoothed his black fur. "What a cutie." His response was to lick her nose. She laughed.

Molly took a seat at the table. "You're getting a good dose of Angus therapy," she said. "He always makes me feel better when I need it." She picked up her mug and sipped her tea, a blend of lavender, vanilla, and chamomile.

For a few minutes, they drank tea and nibbled on cookies. Molly felt the tension seep out of her own body and noticed that Catriona appeared calmer as well. A little color had come into her cheeks and her brow was smoother, not as creased with fear and distress.

Then Catriona gave such a big yawn that it shifted Angus, still sitting on her lap. He gave her a quizzical stare, an expression that made them both laugh. "Sorry, Angus," she said. "All of a sudden I'm completely wiped out."

"Me too," Molly said. She drank the last of her tea. "I'll go get the pullout ready for you." She could hardly wait to crawl into her own bed. This strange, tragic night couldn't end too soon.

7

Wind whistling around the eaves woke Molly the next morning. It disturbed Angus as well, who cuddled closer to her with a groan. Molly glanced at the clock. "Sorry, Angus, but it's time to get up." She sidled past the warm dog and out of the bed, where she fished for a slipper with her foot.

Once she had her slippers on and a robe tied around her middle, she opened the curtains. It was snowing again, and with the low-hanging clouds and the wind whipping off the lake, the dawning day appeared forbidding and grim. The kind of day no one should venture out into—unless they were forced to.

Mindful that she had a guest, Molly heated up some honey-oat muffins in the oven and put on a pot of coffee. Moving to the den door, she tapped lightly. "Catriona? I've got coffee and muffins almost ready."

"Come in," Catriona called.

As Molly cracked the door, Angus dashed past her to the pullout sofa bed. He leaped up to greet their guest.

Catriona laughed, pushing herself to a seated position. "Now this is a way to get woken up." She gave the little dog a thorough rubdown on his neck, making his tags jingle. She glanced up at Molly. "I'll be right out. Thanks for breakfast—and everything else."

"No problem," Molly said. "I'm going to take a quick shower. Shoo him away if he bothers you."

"I wouldn't dream of it." Catriona laughed again as Angus curled up on her legs.

Molly hurried through her morning routine, planning to head down to the bakehouse and give Catriona some privacy. When she came out of the bathroom dressed and ready for her day, she saw Catriona wrapping up a phone call at the table.

"Mr. McNab is on his way," she told Molly. "He said he'll pick me up here and we'll go over to the jail together." She wrapped her arms around herself with a shiver. "The bail hearing is tomorrow morning. So Brodie has to stay in jail another night." Her features twisted in dismay. "Which also means the restaurant will be closed, at least for today and probably tomorrow. Oh, Molly, our lives are falling apart."

Molly hurried over and gave Catriona a hug. "We'll be praying for you and Brodie. Keep us posted, okay?" She saw that Catriona had poured herself a mug of coffee, and that a half-eaten muffin sat on the table. "Feel free to eat whatever you want here or come down for something else."

Sniffing back tears, Catriona picked up the muffin. "This is delicious. Just what I need to settle my nerves." She gave Molly a brave smile, then took another bite.

Molly fully understood the ability of carbs to soothe and comfort. "I'm glad. I'll be downstairs if you need me." She picked up her phone. "You can even send a text if you want. I'll have my phone nearby."

Her guest's smile widened. "Isn't it crazy to text someone in the same building? Brodie and I started doing that too." Then the smile faltered and she dropped her gaze.

"It will be okay," Molly said, with more assurance than she felt. She patted Catriona on the shoulder, said goodbye to Angus, and went down the inner stairs to the bakehouse.

As soon as she stepped into the kitchen, Laura switched off the mixer and pulled the big bowl free. "Good morning. So, about last night . . ." Her voice trailed off and she raised her brows in an inquiring expression.

Molly poured herself a cup of coffee. "I know. I've got a lot to tell you."

The back door opened and Carol entered, a gust of cold air accompanying her. "It's brutal out there today. But Harvey is *still* going fishing."

"I'm sure he'll be warm enough in that hut," Molly said. "Coffee?" At Carol's nod, she filled two more mugs, assuming that Laura would want a cup as well.

"Molly was about to fill me in," Laura said to Carol, who came to join them, reaching for her mug with a smile of gratitude.

"That's right," Carol said. "We didn't get a chance to talk last night." A frown creased her brow. "You and Fergus found Finlay's body?"

Molly perched on a stool. "We sure did." She shook her head to dislodge the image. "But that's not all." She quickly took them through the entire evening, ending with discovering the bow and arrows at Brodie's house.

Both women gasped. "I can't believe it," Laura said. "No way did Brodie kill him."

"I agree," Molly said. "Donal McNab, that defense attorney they call Bulldog, is on his way now to take Catriona over to the jail. She spent the night here with me. She couldn't stay at her house, especially since the police were searching it."

"What a nightmare," Carol said. "I hope Brodie gets out on bail."

Laura leaned against the counter, her mug cradled in her hands. "Me too. What's going to happen to the restaurant if he doesn't? Shutting it down, even temporarily, is not a good idea."

"That's true," Molly agreed. "By the time they reopen, people could be out of the habit of going there." She wrinkled her nose. "Of course, if people think Brodie is guilty of murder, they might not go for that reason."

"It's a tough situation all around." Carol glanced at the clock. "Time to open. I'll go unlock the door."

"I'm right behind you," Molly said.

Laura washed her hands at the sink. "And I'd better get cracking on the vanilla glaze for these peach pie scones. I used those local peaches I froze last July."

"Yum," Carol sang out as she and Molly headed out of the kitchen. "A taste of summer in the middle of winter."

Molly could use more than a taste of summer right now. She closed her eyes for a second and remembered warm breezes off the lake, the pleasure of sunshine touching her face and shoulders. Then she opened her eyes and saw reality, where heaps of snow edged their parking lot, gleaming in the cold, dull light of winter. Good thing their plow service was reliable, or else customers wouldn't be able to get near the bakehouse.

A late model Lexus SUV turned into the driveway, a man at the wheel. While helping Carol with the last-minute setup in the main room, Molly kept an eye on the parking lot. After a moment, a man emerged from the car clutching a buttery-smooth leather briefcase. He wore a trim winter overcoat and a fur-lined hat with flaps. Black leather gloves matched his practical boots.

Donal "Bulldog" McNab had arrived.

Molly went to the door to greet the attorney. "Good morning," she said. "I'm Molly Ferris. Your client is upstairs."

Donal's keen eyes studied Molly's face, and she had a feeling he saw far more than the surface. She'd hate to be a wrongdoer suffering his scrutiny. "Nice to meet you, Mrs. Ferris." He removed his hat, revealing a boyish face and thick red hair. If not for his bearing and reputation, Molly never would have believed he knew his way around a courtroom. He moved his intense gaze to the bakery counter. "Might

I trouble you for coffee and a pastry? I didn't even pause for breakfast this morning."

"Of course. Follow me." Molly put together a tray and carried it upstairs, followed by McNab. Then she left attorney and client alone to talk while she returned to work.

A short while later, she saw the two of them get into his SUV and drive away. "I hope everything goes well," she said to Carol, who was working behind the counter with her.

"As well as it can, visiting your spouse in jail," Carol said grimly.

While Molly waited on a happy couple flirting and laughing over their bagels and coffee, she thought of something—or actually, someone. Jeanne Dupont, Finlay's friend. How was Jeanne doing? Did she have any support during this time of grief?

The front door opened and Fergus came in, doing the usual dance of stamping his boots on the rug before taking off his outerwear. His gaze went right to Molly, who waved. She waited behind the counter for him to approach.

"How are you this morning?" she asked, reaching for a mug to fill his usual coffee order.

Fergus studied the case of pastries. "A bit tired, but it's nothing a large coffee and a scone won't fix."

Laura barged out of the kitchen with a tray. "Want to test these? Peach pie scones with vanilla glaze."

Fergus grinned. "Sold."

Molly grabbed one of the peach scones and put it on a plate, then rang Fergus up.

"Why don't you take a break, Molly?" Carol suggested. "I can handle this." She tipped her chin toward the few customers in the bakehouse. There was a school delay this morning due to the snow, which meant a lot of people in town hadn't ventured out yet.

"Thanks." Molly dispensed a mug of coffee for herself, appreciating the chance to sit with Fergus and chat. She also took a scone, then she and Fergus found a table in the corner. The window next to them revealed fat snowflakes falling nearly sideways on the blustery wind.

"There'll be trees down before too long," Fergus said. "Between the heavy, wet snow and the wind, we might lose power."

"I sure hope not," Molly said, nibbling her scone. The sweet peach flavor was like a burst of sunshine on her tongue—just what she needed on a stormy winter day.

"Did Donal McNab come by yet?" Fergus asked.

"He did," Molly confirmed. "He and Catriona went to the jail to see Brodie." She held up crossed fingers. "And hopefully the judge will set bail and release him at the hearing tomorrow."

"I sincerely hope the police don't consider the case closed. There were plenty of people who had access to that bow and arrows."

"Absolutely. Catriona said the office wasn't locked." Granted, the fact that the weapon was left in Brodie's home probably reduced the number of possible suspects to those who knew where they lived, but that still must be quite a lot of people. Changing the subject, Molly asked, "Do you know where Jeanne Dupont's cabin is? I realized this morning that she probably doesn't have any support."

Fergus shook his head. "She's not staying at the cabin. It's currently winterized, which means the plumbing is shut down so the pipes don't freeze. She has a room at the resort."

"And she's still there?" Molly asked. The poor woman was probably eager to leave town after this tragedy, though the police likely wanted her to remain close during the investigation. Then a suspicion whispered in Molly's ear. Jeanne had left the restaurant first. Had she killed Finlay? Molly shook her head. She shouldn't start suspecting people without proof.

"As far as I know." Fergus picked up his phone and tapped away. "No, she hasn't checked out."

Molly raised an eyebrow, impressed. "You can access your reservation system on your phone?"

"I can oversee a lot of the resort functions with this little device." He smiled as he set the phone down. "It comes in handy when I'm out on the grounds. Or fishing."

Molly pictured him sitting in a boat in the middle of the loch, still able to keep tabs on his business. "That's awesome."

"It is, as long as we have Internet and cell service," he said. "If systems go down, we're reduced to the old-fashioned methods."

"Whatever works." Molly's thoughts returned to Jeanne. "I think I will pop over and see Jeanne later. No one should be alone after a personal tragedy."

Fergus pressed his lips together. "Good point. I'll have the clerk call the room and check on her. Maybe send up breakfast, on the house." He picked up his phone again. "And flowers."

"You're so thoughtful," Molly said, watching as he took care of business. The resort was known for its high quality customer service, and she knew that it was a reflection of the owner's philosophy.

He didn't respond to her compliment, but his smile was warm when he once again set the phone aside. "In other news, the fishing derby is still on, despite the weather. And Vernon accepted my offer to judge."

Molly wrinkled her nose. "You're very brave. Well, dress warmly, that's all I'm going to say." Her gaze strayed again to the snow and ice outside. "This weather is positively wicked."

After the bakehouse closed, the women climbed into Carol's Chrysler, Laura toting a small box of baked goodies, and headed out to the resort to visit Jeanne.

The snow had stopped and the roads were now mostly clear. Carol drove slowly to avoid patches of ice and the slushy margins on the side of the road, which could grab a tire and yank a car into the ditch in the blink of an eye.

Although Castleglen was only two miles from downtown, the journey felt much longer. Not only was Molly concerned about the roads, but she was nervous about their meeting with Jeanne. How would the woman react? She really had no idea if they would be welcome or not. In times of grief—or guilt—people were often unpredictable.

She let out a relieved sigh as Carol navigated through the resort's welcoming gates and onto the recently plowed driveway. After a short distance, the stone-and-wood main building appeared, the lights twinkling golden in the quickly darkening afternoon. Carol continued past the main entrance and found a spot in the visitor's parking area.

Inside the lobby, Molly spotted Fergus's son, Neil, talking to the young woman working at the desk. The younger MacGregor was learning the ropes at the resort, and Fergus often praised his son's work ethic and aptitude for hospitality.

"Good afternoon," Neil said, smiling at the trio as they approached. "It's good to see you again."

At this signal that her boss knew the women, the clerk's attentive expression brightened. "How may I help you?" she asked.

"We're here to see Jeanne Dupont," Molly said. "Could you please call up and ask if she's willing to accept visitors?" She gave their names to the clerk, who nodded and picked up the phone.

"Hasn't the weather been awful?" Neil asked the women while the clerk was on the phone. "We can barely keep up with plowing and sanding."

Almost everyone in town was talking about Finlay's murder, but Molly appreciated that Neil was being so discreet. It wouldn't create a very nice atmosphere to be discussing such a gruesome topic in the lobby, she reflected, where anyone might overhear. Even the nearby television was set to the weather station rather than local news, the volume muted so as not to compete with the gentle music piped over the intercom.

"You're doing a nice job, Neil," Carol said. "The parking lot wasn't a bit slippery. I can't say the same for sidewalks downtown."

"I'm glad to hear that," Neil said. "We want our guests to be safe." His face fell briefly, no doubt thinking of Finlay, but then the charming smile reappeared. "Dad called me a while ago. He's over at the fishing derby. He mentioned that Harvey did really well today."

Carol beamed. "That's great. Harvey does love his fishing."

The clerk hung up. "Ms. Dupont would be happy to have you visit her. She's in room 306."

The Bakehouse Three thanked the clerk and Neil for their assistance, then hurried across the lobby to the elevator. The car swept them silently to the third floor, where they exited into a hushed hallway. Not for the first time, Molly marveled at how tasteful, relaxing, and elegant everything at Castleglen was as they walked down the hallway and watched for room 306.

"Here it is," Laura said, stopping in front of a door. She knocked three times.

With a click of the lock, the door opened to reveal Jeanne, who was bundled in a thick wool sweater, fleece leggings, and big slippers. Dark circles under her eyes and a reddened nose marred her face. In one hand, she clutched a bundle of tissues. "Come in," she said, her voice nasal.

The women filed into the room, which was spacious, furnished with a large bed, a long bureau, and a seating area with a sofa and accent table that had a bouquet of flowers on it. The television on the wall was playing a local news show, and Jeanne snatched up the remote to mute the volume.

"Do you want some coffee?" Jeanne asked. "I can make a pot." She moved toward the kitchenette tucked into a corner.

"Perfect," Laura said. "We brought you some goodies." She gestured with the box before setting it on the table beside the floral arrangement.

"How lovely," Jeanne said, hands clasped and blinking back tears. "You all are so thoughtful." She used the tissue to dab at her eyes. "Sorry. I wasn't really expecting all this."

"Why don't you have a seat?" Carol guided Jeanne to the sofa. "We can take care of the coffee." She went over to the kitchenette and opened a cabinet door, looking for mugs.

Jeanne didn't argue as she flopped onto the sofa. "Thanks. I have no energy right now, which is not like me."

"It's the shock," Laura said, opening the bakery box. "Have you eaten today?"

The professor shook her head. "I couldn't." She patted her midriff. "After I heard the news, it felt like everything knotted up into a big ball."

Molly totally understood. She had experienced devastating losses of her own, including her husband, Kevin, several years earlier. "Try a scone." She retrieved a peach scone and placed it on a napkin, then put the treat on the end table next to Jeanne. "They're very soothing, and I've heard that sugar is good for shock."

Someone knocked on the room door and a woman's voice called, "Housekeeping."

Jeanne turned in her seat. "Oh, can you let her in? I asked for some extra towels."

"Of course." Carol, who was closest, went to the door and opened it. "Want me to take those?" she asked.

"No thanks," came the answer. "I'm going to take away the used ones."

Carol stepped aside, and a woman in her forties entered. She had fine dark hair gathered in a ponytail and startling light blue eyes.

"Tara?" Jeanne shot to her feet. "What in the world are you doing here?"

8

The newcomer took a step back, glancing in both directions. "I work here." Tara's eyebrows knit. "I didn't know you were staying here, Jeanne." She clutched the stack of white towels to her chest.

"My cabin is still winterized," Jeanne said. She edged past Molly. "Did you hear the news?"

Confusion clouded Tara's face. "About what?"

Jeanne crossed her arms, regarding the other woman skeptically. "Finlay's dead," she said bluntly. "Last night. I can't believe you don't know."

Tara's mouth dropped open, her features working as she obviously struggled to accept this news. Then she thrust the towels toward Carol, muttered "I'm sorry," and ran out of the room.

Molly, Laura, and Carol exchanged startled glances. Then the door slammed behind Tara, reanimating everyone. Carol deposited the towels in the bathroom, Laura sat down with Jeanne, and Molly went to the kitchenette and poured the coffee.

"What was that all about?" Laura asked. "I take it she knew Finlay?"

Jeanne's lip curled. "She used to work as his administrative assistant at the college." She hesitated before adding, "But he fired her. And now she's a maid in a hotel." The shake of her head revealed that she considered Tara's new job a demotion.

"That's too bad," Carol said, rejoining the group. "It's never an easy situation to lose a job. Or to be the one firing someone."

Under normal circumstances, Molly would feel bad about Tara's humiliation. But now this revelation made her wonder—had Tara resented Finlay? Maybe she felt he had fired her unjustly. Molly set Jeanne's mug on the side table, along with a creamer and two sugar packets.

"In all fairness to Tara," Jeanne added, nodding thanks at Molly, "Finlay wasn't the easiest person to work for. He could be very particular." She picked up the creamer and peeled back the top. "He fired more than one assistant."

"You seemed surprised to see Tara working here," Laura said.

"I certainly was," Jeanne said. "I had no idea she'd moved away from Marquette. But it makes sense considering that her son, Noah, is living here too."

"I've met Noah," Molly said. "He was helping at the fishing tournament. He's also a server at Neeps and Tatties."

Jeanne made a tsk-tsk sound. "Oh, Noah. Now there's a sad case."

"What do you mean?" Laura asked.

"Noah was a top student at the college," Jeanne said. "On the dean's list and everything. And then he dropped out right before graduation last May."

"That's awful. Why in the world did he do that?" Molly hated hearing about young people whose lives took a downturn. She was so grateful that her daughter, Chloe, had excelled in college and was now a happy and successful veterinarian, her dream job.

Jeanne shrugged. "I'm not sure. The whole thing was very hush-hush. I do know Finlay was terribly disappointed in Noah. He regarded him as something of a protégé."

Molly's pulse rate jumped. Both Noah and Tara must have known Finlay quite well. She made a mental note to call Chief Thomson after they left the resort.

"So many people from Marquette are here this week," Carol

mused, her thoughts obviously running along the same lines as Molly's. She sipped the coffee Molly had handed her.

The professor barked a laugh. "You're so right. You could have knocked me over with a feather when I saw Sheldon and Sheila at the historical society meeting the other night. I had no idea they had moved up here either."

"You already knew them?" Laura asked. "Wow, that is a coincidence."

Molly was starting to think she should make a chart to keep track of the relationships. "How do you know the Barkers? Were you an insurance client?"

Jeanne's lips curved in a smile. "No, but not for lack of Sheldon trying. I actually knew Sheila first. We met at a women's outdoor adventure weekend. You know, camping, kayaking, fishing, archery..." At the mention of archery, her voice trailed off and her gaze dropped.

An uneasy silence fell. "So," Molly said, to fill the quiet. "Sheila is quite the outdoorswoman. I wouldn't have guessed it." *Both women know how to use a bow and arrow? I'm definitely giving the chief a call.*

"She wasn't very good," Jeanne admitted. "At any of it. But she was game to try, and that's what counts, right?"

Molly moved Sheila down on the suspect list, but then reconsidered. Maybe the insurance agent's wife had improved her archery skills since that weekend with Jeanne.

"She's certainly got diverse interests," Carol said. "Her portrait of Burns was quite unique. And how nice of her to donate it for the Burns Week."

Jeanne apparently disagreed. "That thing is hideous. Robert Burns would roll over in his grave if he saw it."

As Molly was trying to find a way to defend Sheila's artistry, Carol's phone dinged. She pulled it from her pocket and read something, then grinned. "Harvey caught the biggest fish today." As Molly and Laura chorused congratulations, Carol sent back a text.

"Harvey's your husband?" Jeanne asked. "He has the best laugh. I remember noticing it at the restaurant. It rang out above the clatter."

Carol smiled. "Yes, he's got a real belly laugh. Even after all these years, it makes me happy whenever I hear it."

"You're so lucky," Jeanne said, obvious envy in her tone. She began to blink back tears. "I wanted that with Finlay. Being an old married couple, the laughs, the annoyances."

Molly laid a sympathetic hand on Jeanne's arm. "I'm so sorry, Jeanne. Were you planning on getting married?"

Jeanne flopped back against the sofa cushions with a huff. "Not exactly. I wanted to—I mean, we'd been dating five whole years—but Finlay had the coldest feet you ever saw. After his divorce about a million years ago, he vowed to never get married again." Her face crumpled. "Now we'll never get our happily ever after."

An hour later, Molly, Laura, and Carol were finally on their way toward the front entrance. They hadn't wanted to leave Jeanne alone in her obvious grief. But beyond the professor's understandable sorrow, there had been a bitterness that concerned Molly. Jeanne was firmly on the ever-growing list of suspects.

As they crossed the lobby, Fergus came through the double doors. The tips of his nose and ears were red and his boots were covered in snow. "Good afternoon," he said. "Were you visiting Jeanne?"

"Yep, and we sure got an earful up there," Laura said, her expression rueful. "A lot of people resented Finlay."

"Interesting," Fergus said, his eyes widening with curiosity. "If you have a moment, want to step into my office and give me an update?"

The three quickly agreed and followed Fergus to his office, where he shed his outerwear then ushered them to a table with four chairs.

"Would you like coffee or tea?" he asked.

"Thanks, but I'm all set," Molly said. "We had coffee with Jeanne."

Neither Laura nor Carol wanted coffee either, so Fergus made himself a cup in the single-serving maker.

"Your husband did great today," Fergus said to Carol as he joined them at the table, a mug of steaming coffee in one hand.

"I heard," Carol said. "He texted me. He was over the moon."

"It was a good day overall." Fergus smiled. "No fights." A serious expression replaced his grin. "So tell me what you learned."

With interjections from Laura and Carol, Molly took Fergus through the events of the afternoon. "I want to call the chief and tell him what we learned," she concluded. "These three people—Noah, Tara, and Jeanne—had reason to resent Finlay. And they certainly knew him better than Brodie did. Plus, Jeanne was hurt because Finlay wouldn't marry her. Remember, she left the restaurant before he did."

"Those are all very good points." Fergus pulled a landline telephone sitting on the table a little closer. "Why don't we give him a call right now?"

"Sure." Molly nodded, pleased that Fergus believed them. His support could only lend credibility to their theories.

Fergus picked up the receiver and dialed. When the call was answered, he identified himself and asked for the chief. A few seconds later, he said, "Hello, Chief. Molly, Carol, and Laura are with me in my office. I'm going to put you on speaker."

"Hello, everyone." Chief Thomson's voice boomed out over the speakerphone. "What's going on?"

Fergus gestured for Molly to answer. "Good afternoon, Chief.

This is Molly. We were visiting Jeanne Dupont this afternoon and we learned some interesting things."

"Jeanne Dupont?" The chief's tone sharpened. "Finlay's friend?"

"Yes," Molly said. "We felt bad that she was all alone here in town, so we took her some baked goods."

The chief sighed audibly. "How many times do I need to ask you ladies to stay out of my investigations?"

"We were worried about her," Carol protested.

"I'm sure," Thomson said, and Molly could practically see him shaking his head. "All right, you wouldn't be calling unless you learned something. Better tell me what it is."

Once again Molly and the other women shared what they had learned about Finlay's relationships. "I know that Brodie's equipment was used to kill Finlay," Molly concluded. "But Jeanne has experience with a bow and arrow, and so does Sheila Barker. Although she doesn't seem to have a motive." She thought of something else. "And those fishermen who were at the dinner. They didn't like Finlay either after the way he acted at the fishing tournament. Maybe they do archery too."

After Molly finished speaking, Fergus said, "As you can see, Chief, there are a lot of people who disliked Finlay Croft. I'm certainly not going to tell you how to do your job, but isn't it possible that one of them killed him rather than Brodie?"

The chief was silent for a long moment. "I'm taking everything you've said under advisement. But I do want to make one thing clear. We arrested Brodie McCauley based on evidence, not opinion. However, as we continue our investigation, we will certainly review any new information with an open mind."

"That's all we ask," Fergus said. "We appreciate your time." They said their goodbyes, and Fergus ended the call. "There you have it. Ball's in his court now."

"And we will certainly make sure that Donal McNab hears about these other possible suspects," Carol said. "I'm sure it seemed like a cut-and-dried case to the district attorney, but it certainly is not."

"No, it's quite the opposite," Laura said. "So many people had access to that bow and arrow in an unlocked office. And everyone who resented Finlay was at Neeps and Tatties that night. Well, except for Tara."

"And she could have entered the restaurant while everyone was busy in the dining room," Molly said. "She or anybody else could have gone down the hall to the office without being noticed."

"Maybe Tara grabbed the bow and arrows, then lurked in the parking lot until Finlay left the restaurant," Carol suggested.

The phone on the table beeped. "Fergus, are you there?" a voice said over the intercom.

"I am," he replied. "Hang on, I'll be right with you."

Carol rose to her feet. "I guess that's our cue. It was good to see you, Fergus, and thanks for listening."

"Anytime." Fergus opened the office door for the Bakehouse Three. "Keep me posted if you learn anything new." He smiled at Molly, who was last to leave the room. "See you in the morning for coffee."

"I'm so nervous," Catriona whispered, grabbing Molly by the forearm.

The Bakehouse Three were attending the midmorning bail hearing at the courthouse while Hamish and Bridget held down the fort at Bread on Arrival.

"We're here for you," Molly assured the younger woman. She glanced around at the packed hallway. "And so are a lot of other

Loch Mallaig residents." No Fergus, though. He had come by for coffee when the bakehouse opened, but then had been needed at the fishing tournament.

Catriona squeezed her eyes shut for a moment as she inhaled slowly. "Okay, I'm ready. Let's go in." Carried along with the throng, they entered the courtroom and found seats together close to the front.

The room was noisy with chatter until the judge was announced, which caused a hush to fall over the assembly. As a bailiff brought Brodie in, dressed in orange and handcuffed, the tension in the room rose even higher. Catriona, sitting between Molly and Carol, squeezed their hands so tightly it hurt. But Molly didn't protest, feeling instead a deep sympathy for Catriona's ordeal. What if that was her husband being brought before a judge in a packed courtroom? She shuddered, imagining it. She noticed that the media were there too, reporters scribbling away in notebooks or on tablets. This was a big news story in the Upper Peninsula.

Stern, raven-haired Judge Constance Bedford banged her gavel, announcing that proceedings were to begin. Molly watched in a daze, barely taking in the words of the prosecutor and Donal McNab, or Judge Bedford's responses. Her every nerve was focused on the issue of bail, which would be brought up soon. She truly believed that somehow justice would prevail and Finlay's real killer would be unmasked. But in the meantime, it was better for Brodie to be home with his wife, not languishing in a jail cell.

Finally the moment came. Donal addressed the judge. "Your Honor," he said in a tone that was precisely the right mix of confident and reasonable for a no-nonsense judge like this. "We are requesting that bail be set to allow Brodie McCauley to await trial at home. As a well-established businessman, he has very strong ties to the community, including his family and many friends."

He paused to let the judge absorb that, then went on. "He's never had so much as a parking ticket. In fact, having formerly worked as a fireman in Chicago and currently serving as the Loch Mallaig Volunteer Fire Company chief, he's a hero. Brodie was honored by the mayor of Chicago for risking his own life while saving small children trapped in a deadly high-rise fire."

Molly hadn't been aware of Brodie's commendation—he wasn't the type to brag, after all. Her esteem for the man rose a notch, and she sensed that others in the room were also impressed. She now had an even harder time believing that such a man would kill another in cold blood.

"Surely a man like this, a family man, an employer, a hero, can be trusted to stay in the country and out of trouble," Donal concluded, his freckled face earnest.

The prosecutor made a token protest. "I'm concerned about flight to Canada, your Honor," he said. "The border is mere miles away."

Donal made a scoffing sound, as if the idea of Brodie fleeing the country was absurd. "As a sign of good faith, my client will happily surrender his passport for the time being."

Catriona's grip grew stronger as they waited for the judge's decision. When Judge Bedford finally announced the bail, she released their hands and burst into tears. At the sound, Brodie glanced over his shoulder, his expression both troubled and yearning. Molly thought it was touching that he recognized the sound of his wife crying. She hoped that it wouldn't be a recurring experience for the couple.

"There, you see?" Carol soothed, handing Catriona a tissue. "You'll be reunited in no time."

After wiping her tears away, Catriona gave them each a hug. "Come by the restaurant tonight. We won't be officially open, but we'll be serving dinner for friends. At least that's what I'm going to suggest to Brodie. I'm sure he'll be up for it."

"Sounds great," Laura said. "I'll bake a cake."

"With a file in it?" Catriona joked, smiling for the first time that morning. "Oh, that's right, we won't need one." She gave them each another hug, then headed down the aisle. The paperwork would take a while to process, and she was going to wait with Donal for Brodie's official release.

Molly smiled as she walked toward the door, grateful that Brodie wouldn't spend another day in jail. Her happiness faltered, however, when she realized the grim truth—to make sure he wouldn't return to prison, they'd have to redouble their efforts to uncover Finlay's true killer.

9

"**W**hat do you think?" Laura asked Molly. They were standing in the bakehouse kitchen, getting ready to head across the street to Neeps and Tatties. Laura had made a three-layer cake and decorated it with Scottie dogs, thistles, and a strip of black-and-green McCauley plaid made from painted fondant. *When friends meet, hearts warm*, an old Scottish proverb, was piped on top.

"It's a masterpiece," Molly said. "Just gorgeous." Since Carol was the bakery's cake maven, she often forgot that Laura's decorating skills matched their third partner's. She picked up her phone and took a few snaps for Bread on Arrival's social media pages. "We definitely need to post pictures, show the world what you can do."

Laura grinned, striking a pose with the cake. "Aw shucks."

After Laura packed the cake in a carrier, they bundled up for the outdoors, even though they were only going across the street. It wasn't snowing, but the winds were gusty and the temperature was dropping. With heads bent against the blast, they hurried over to the restaurant.

No cars were in the lot other than Brodie's truck. That gave her pause, as did the sign saying *Closed*. But the door opened when Molly pulled on it, so she held it for Laura.

"We must be early," Molly murmured. "Or else the gathering was canceled."

"I know the Robert Burns poetry slam is being held at Superior Bay College tonight," Laura said. "But I think it was mostly geared toward students."

"Maybe there are more amateur poets among us than we thought."

"It'd be a shame if everyone went to that instead," Laura said. "But I'll leave the cake anyway."

The swinging door to the kitchen opened and Catriona backed out, carrying a pan with oven-mitted hands. "I thought I heard someone. Come on in."

Molly and Laura followed her to the buffet table along the wall, where trays and platters of food were lined up. It all smelled heavenly. "Wow, what a spread."

Catriona slid the pan into a holder above a flame. "Guess what Brodie's been doing all day, ever since we got home?" She glanced toward the restaurant entrance. "And now I hope everyone shows up."

"Where should we put the cake?" Laura asked.

"Right here." Catriona led the way to a smaller table for desserts. Coffee and hot water urns were already plugged in. She gasped as Laura unpacked the cake and put it in the center of the table. "That is incredible."

"Thanks," Laura said, her cheeks reddening. "It was fun to make."

Brodie burst out of the kitchen, pushing a cart that held a huge roast beef. He wheeled toward them, intent on his task. But when he got to the buffet table, he glanced up and said, "Where is everyone?"

Catriona's brow furrowed. "I don't know." She glanced at the wall clock. "We did say six, right?" It was now a quarter after.

Brodie eyed the array of food with a rueful expression. "If no one comes, we're sure going to have a lot of leftovers."

Molly's heart ached for the poor man, who was probably wondering if his friends had abandoned him. She stepped aside and pulled out her phone. She quickly sent Carol and Fergus a text. *At Neeps and Tatties. Where are you?*

Leaving now, Fergus shot right back.

Carol, who had gone home to pick up Harvey, wrote, *We're just pulling in.*

"People are on their way," Molly said, feeling lighter with relief. Car tires crunched in the parking lot, followed by the sound of slamming doors. "Here they come."

The couple burst into action, trading instructions. Catriona thrust water pitchers at Laura. "Do you mind filling these? Use the ice machine behind the bar. And Molly, can you grab a tray of napkin-wrapped silverware from the kitchen?"

As Molly and Laura hurried to do Catriona's bidding, the restaurant doors burst open and a stream of guests poured in. By the time Molly returned from the kitchen with the silverware, Alastair Thomson was playing a jig on his bagpipes while Catriona lit a fire in the big fireplace. A party atmosphere began to build in the room, fueled by laughter and chatter.

As for Brodie, he was swamped by warm greetings. Even the usually dour Vernon Pennycook had a slap on the shoulder and a kind word for the beleaguered fireman.

Fergus appeared at Molly's side as she placed rolls of utensils next to a stack of plates. Dressed nicely in a black turtleneck under a trim gray plaid blazer, he greeted her with a smile, then asked, "How are you tonight?"

She paused in her work and returned the smile. "Great now that I know the party isn't a bust. How about you?"

He adjusted his jacket sleeves while glancing around at the growing crowd. "I'm doing well, thanks. Sorry I was late, but we had a problem with the generator. It needed to be dealt with because we're supposed to get really high winds tonight and without the backup generator, we'd be sunk."

"Uncomfortable guests and ruined perishables in the restaurant refrigerators would certainly be problematic," Molly said. "You got it fixed?"

Fergus nodded. "Thankfully."

Brodie tapped a spoon on a glass and the room fell silent. "I want to thank you all for coming out on such a raw, unpleasant night. And I'm only talking about my personal problems." Everyone roared with laughter. The tension etching Brodie's features relaxed a trifle. "So let's eat."

The crowd moved toward the buffet table, forming a line. Soon they were all seated with heaping plates in front of them. As Molly settled at a table with Laura, Carol, Harvey, and Fergus, she glanced around to see who else was there. She spotted many members of the historical society, the Barkers, and Noah Taggart and his mother, Tara. Noah wasn't working tonight, and he was sitting with other Neeps and Tatties employees.

Brodie and Catriona had set everything up for casual self-service, so once their guests were eating, they filled plates for themselves and joined Molly's table.

"How is everything?" Brodie asked.

"Delicious," Carol said with a laugh. "Can't you tell? We're barely talking."

Harvey, who had a huge slab of roast beef on his plate, nodded agreement as he chewed.

Brodie's question set the tone for dinner conversation, and all discussion of Finlay, Brodie's courtroom visit, and the future was avoided while they ate. A hot topic for Fergus and Harvey was the fishing derby.

"At least it gives us old guys something to do," Harvey said. "Otherwise I'd be watching too much television and going stir-crazy."

"Maybe I'll join you on the lake one day this week," Brodie said. "I haven't gone fishing for years, though I used to enjoy it with Uncle Jock."

Catriona tilted her head. "So you're serious about shutting down for a while?"

Her husband shrugged. "I thought maybe we wouldn't get any customers." His eyes flitted about the crowded room. "But it could be I was wrong."

"You've got a lot of friends in this town," Fergus said. He held up his fork, which had speared a hunk of juicy beef. "And fabulous food. What will we do if you're closed?"

Brodie grinned. "That's high praise coming from you, Fergus. Your restaurants are top-notch."

"Right back at you," Fergus said lightly. He swirled the piece of beef in gravy and popped it into his mouth.

"You can share my bob-house if you want, Brodie," Harvey said. "It's a little tight in there, but two can fish okay."

"Thanks, Harvey." Brodie glanced around the room. "Looks like people are ready for dessert."

Catriona put a hand on his arm. "Sit. Coffee and hot water are ready. They can all help themselves."

Laura rose from the table. "I'm going up to make the first cuts in the cake."

"Did you see the cake Laura made, Brodie?" Catriona asked. "It's lovely."

"I did." Brodie smiled up at Laura, then at Molly and Carol. "You three are the best. It's wonderful having the bakehouse right across the street. So convenient when you have a craving for something sweet."

"And we send a lot of people over here," Carol said, "since we don't serve meals."

"A real win-win," Catriona declared. She hopped up. "I'm going to get us cake. Want coffee, Brodie?"

Carol and Harvey also headed up for dessert, which left Fergus and Molly alone at the table with Brodie. The fireman was still working his way through his dinner, as were Molly and Fergus. She was thoroughly enjoying a slice of meat pie with a golden crust and savory filling.

"I'll never take anything for granted again," Brodie said. He waved a hand at the room. "I loved my job as a fireman, but when Uncle Jock was dying, taking over this place seemed like the right thing to do." His mouth curved in a smile. "All those nights cooking at the firehouse helped me perfect my recipes."

"I've heard about the great meals firefighters prepare on shift," Molly said.

Brodie nodded. "Wards off boredom while we're waiting for a call. Granted, a lot of meals get cold when the call does come in."

"Do you miss the excitement?" she asked.

"Nope," was the brief reply. "I was ready for a change. And I still get a chance to use my skills with the local fire company. Fortunately, the occasional overzealous bonfire or leaky gas oven isn't quite as intimidating as some of the calls I used to go out on. Catriona wouldn't say it, but I know a couple of the bigger fires rattled her nerves."

"I can understand that," Molly said, thinking how hard it must have been for Catriona to say goodbye to her husband when he went to work, knowing that he might never return. Now the couple faced a huge threat to their happiness from a new challenge—a possible murder conviction. Molly could hardly bear it.

"I can't believe someone used my bow and arrow to kill Finlay." Brodie's voice dropped to almost a whisper. "It's so rotten."

"It sure is," Fergus said. "Especially considering your supposed motive is really weak. They think you did it to avenge your uncle, right?"

Molly's eyebrows went up. She hadn't heard this tidbit.

Brodie's expression was glum. "There's more to that story than you probably know. Finlay and Uncle Jock didn't only have a falling-out. Finlay got him tied up in a failed business deal that cost him tens of thousands of dollars. At one point, Uncle Jock almost lost the restaurant—on top of his life savings. When Cat and I bought this place, it was partially so that he actually had money to retire."

"That's terrible." Molly was shocked by this sad tale, but she still thought the motive was thin. "Still, Finlay cost your uncle money, not you."

"I know." Brodie placed his knife and fork neatly on the edge of his plate. "I guess the prosecutor doesn't care, in light of the physical evidence." He set his napkin on the table. "Now, if you'll excuse me, I'm going to see if Cat needs any help."

Fergus turned to Molly. "Want dessert? I can bring you something."

Molly shook her head. "I want answers," she said. "And for Brodie to be cleared."

"Me too," Fergus said gently. "In the meantime, though, a little cake and coffee won't hurt."

Molly glanced at her plate, which still held the remains of meat pie and salad. "Probably not. But honestly, I can't eat another bite. Ask Laura to save me a slice of cake."

After the meal was cleared away, Alastair took up the bagpipes again. After he played a few tunes, one of the Neeps and Tatties employees pulled out a guitar and led an informal sing-along. The fire roared, hot drinks and dessert plates were replenished often—Molly even managed a piece of Laura's delicious cake after all—and all in all, the mood was festive.

Outside the warm restaurant, however, all was grim. The promised wind began to howl around the eaves, blowing powdery snow into the air like streams of confetti. People began to take their leave, hoping to reach their homes before the storm got too bad. Molly, who lived across the street, lingered until only Fergus and their hosts remained.

An especially big gust shook the building and the lights flickered. "Uh-oh," Brodie said. "Here we go."

Catriona hurried to light some candles. The moment she finished, there was another flicker and then the lights were out. Red exit signs lit up at the front door and above the back hallway. The candles provided pools of light.

Molly shuddered.

Fergus checked his phone. "Still good at the resort, thankfully."

"Must have been local then," Brodie said. "Probably a tree down on the wires."

Molly peered out the window toward the bakehouse, which was now in darkness. She'd have to use her phone's flashlight to guide her home, otherwise she would be groping in the dark.

"I can escort you home, if you want." Fergus joined her at the window. "It looks like the whole street is out." He lowered his voice. "But before we go, I'd like to talk to Brodie for a minute."

"That's fine with me," Molly said, relieved that she would have company even if it was a very short journey home.

Brodie was prodding the fire. "I don't like to leave this going," he said.

"You're welcome to stay for a last hot drink," Catriona said. "We often finish the night like this, sitting together in front of the fire. Chai tea, coffee, or regular tea?"

Fergus and Molly opted for chai tea.

"Tonight was really fun," Molly said, taking one of the chairs Brodie pulled close to the fire. How different she felt compared to the night Finlay had died, when she'd huddled near the fire in shock and fear. The gathering's goodwill and friendship seemed to have washed those feelings away, like awakening to sunshine after a bad dream.

Brodie coaxed a few more flames out of the waning embers. "I hope the outage doesn't last long. We've had enough of frozen pipes already this winter."

"I hear you," Fergus said, smiling gratefully at Catriona when she handed him a mug.

After giving Molly her own tea, Catriona sat next to her, releasing a sigh. "It feels so good to sit down."

Brodie stretched his legs toward the fire. "I can't wait until this is all over. I'll never take simple pleasures like this for granted again."

His wife immediately appeared anxious, gnawing at her bottom lip. She glanced at Molly, her eyes glistening with fear.

Fergus shifted in his seat, leaning forward and propping his elbows on his knees. "We're behind you all the way, Brodie. In fact, Molly here has identified three new suspects, and we told the chief about them."

Both McCauleys turned to Molly with looks of surprise. "How did that happen?" Catriona asked. "I know you're a bit of a sleuth, but I didn't realize you were investigating for us."

Molly ducked her head, somewhat embarrassed by the attention. "I'm not a sleuth, honestly. But sometimes I, um, stumble on the truth." She laughed. "And I guess I'm pretty nosy too."

"And we're grateful," Fergus said with an admiring smile. "If Molly wasn't such a good businesswoman, she would have made a great detective."

"Now you're just being silly," Molly told him. Sensing that Brodie was bursting with curiosity about the suspects, she said, "Jeanne Dupont, Tara Taggart, and Noah Taggart all had reason to resent Finlay."

Catriona gasped. "Noah? I had no idea he knew the man."

Molly nodded. "He was a student at the college where Finlay taught. He dropped out suddenly. Finlay was one of his professors."

"But that doesn't mean he hated Finlay," Catriona protested.

"I know," Molly said. "That's why the police—"

A door slammed in the back of the restaurant, startling everyone. An icy shiver jolted down Molly's spine. She'd thought they were alone. Had someone been lurking in the restaurant?

Someone with sinister intent?

10

Brodie shot up straight at the banging sound. "What was that?" Fear crept into his expression. "I thought we were the only people here."

The two men jumped to their feet and bolted for the back hallway. Catriona and Molly followed.

"Was the back door unlocked?" Molly asked. She wondered if someone had been hiding instead of leaving or if they had quietly crept in unseen.

"It's usually only locked from the outside," Catriona said. "We always leave it open while people are here."

The two men were in the hallway, peering out the rear door Brodie had pushed open. Cold air poured in, making Molly shiver.

"I don't see anyone," Fergus said. "Whoever it was took off."

"I'm going to get a flashlight and check it out." Brodie went into the office and reappeared in a moment holding a long metal flashlight.

"I'm coming with you," Fergus volunteered. Although neither man wore a coat, they stepped outside into the parking lot, using a doorstop to prop the heavy door open. Through the doorway, Molly could see the sweep of the beam as Brodie searched the area.

"They're going to freeze," Catriona said, hugging her arms around her middle.

Although they shivered, neither woman moved to close the door. Molly's heart pounded as she waited for them to return. What if someone was lurking out there, ready to kill again? *Be careful!* she wanted to shout, but the words were stuck in her throat.

The men returned a few minutes later, stamping their feet and expressing disappointment. "Whoever it was, he's gone," Brodie said, yanking on the door and letting it slam shut. The sound echoed the one they'd all heard earlier, and Molly was convinced someone had been there.

"Brrr," Fergus said, rubbing his hands together. He looked at Molly. "I need to warm up, but then we'll get you home, okay?"

"Take as long as you need," Molly agreed. Now she was gladder than ever to have Fergus escort her. Then a pang of fear for Fergus struck. "As long as you drive me over so you aren't walking back across the street and through the parking lot alone."

The foursome stood around the fire, doing their best to get warm. Then, to Molly's huge relief, the lights flickered and came on. The furnace in the basement kicked into action with a rumble. Outside the window, streetlights popped on, their welcome glow illuminating the deserted street.

A short while later, Fergus drove Molly home, both of them chuckling at the short distance. "Better safe than sorry," Fergus commented as he parked, leaving the engine running. "I'm going to walk you up."

He followed Molly up the outside staircase and waited while she unlocked the door. Angus sniffed and whined on the other side.

"He misses you," Fergus said.

"Always. Whether it's five minutes or five hours." Molly shook her head with a laugh. She stepped into her apartment, glad that she'd left a couple of lamps on. All was peaceful. "Good night, Fergus. Thank you again for making sure I got home safely."

"Good night," he echoed. "See you at the community center tomorrow night?"

"Wouldn't miss it," Molly said. She and Fergus were both in The

Piping Yoopers, who were going to play Scottish folk songs written or collected by Robert Burns. The Leaping Lowlanders would be performing to the music.

"Until then, if not before," Fergus said in parting, then descended the steps to the yard.

Molly and Angus watched out the window as Fergus got into his Range Rover and drove away. The wind was still blowing hard, whipping bare tree branches about. As Molly stared into the night, she thought she saw a dark figure standing by the trunk of a thick maple. Or was it only her imagination? Although she peered into the dark until Fergus's taillights disappeared, she couldn't be sure if someone was lurking.

She double-checked all the locks, upstairs and down, before going to bed.

After the bakehouse closed the next day, Carol and Laura joined Molly in the apartment, where the trio dressed for the evening's event. Harvey, who had been fishing, was planning to meet Carol at the community center. Angus watched from his spot curled up on Molly's bed.

"It's fun to get dressed up once in a while," Molly said, fastening a tartan sash with a brooch. She was also wearing a white blouse and a full-length tartan skirt. Like the other two, she planned to change her boots to gillies—a traditional lace-up shoe—once they got there. There would be lots of dancing tonight and the soft, flexible gillies were perfect for that.

Laura ran a brush through her auburn hair. "Totally agree. I'm excited to watch Bridget dance. She told me The Leaping Lowlanders have been rehearsing like crazy."

"I spent all afternoon practicing the songs we're playing," Molly said. "I hope my piping didn't drive you or the customers crazy."

"No, we loved it," Laura said. "You should play in the shop sometime."

Molly fluffed out her skirt, checking her reflection in a full-length mirror. "After another couple of years, maybe. I think the walls muffled my worst mistakes."

Carol spritzed on some heather fragrance then offered the bottle to the others. "We're going to have a great time, no doubt about it." Her voice held an edge of determination.

"In spite of Brodie being a murder suspect, you mean?" Laura asked. "I can barely stop thinking about it."

For a moment, a somber mood dropped over the women. "Well, we gave the chief plenty to think about," Molly said to break the silence.

"Your story about the prowler at Neeps and Tatties sure creeped me out," Carol said, tucking the small bottle of scent into her black velvet clutch. "I consider that proof that someone else did it. Why else would they lurk around, trying to eavesdrop?"

"What's worse," Molly said, straightening one leg of her stockings, "is that if they hadn't let the door slam, we wouldn't have known they were there."

Laura shuddered. "Very scary. I'm glad you made it home all right."

Molly gave the stocking a final tug. "Me too. Fortunately Fergus was there as backup. I still think the person was hanging around watching us."

"We'd better stick together, ladies," Carol said, wagging a finger at Laura and Molly. She used the tone that had kept many a rebellious teen in line during her years as a high school math teacher. "No one goes off alone until this is over, understood?"

Laura threw a smiling glance at Molly. "Yes, Mrs. MacCallan."

The Bakehouse Three rode to the community center in Laura's VW Beetle since Harvey had dropped Carol off that morning so she could go home with him. Molly sat in the back, her bagpipes case taking up most of the rear seat.

Cars filled the lot and the streets around the center. At the sight of the crowd, the knot of trepidation in Molly's belly grew to monster size. She felt that way before every performance, a mixture of anxiety and excitement. "Could you please let me out here?" she asked as Laura crept past a side door. "The Yoopers are gathering in a back room."

"Break a leg," Carol said, getting out so Molly could climb out with her instrument case.

Molly waved, then trudged across the icy pavement to the door. She entered into a short hallway lined with doors. The main room was straight ahead, and she could hear the chatter of people gathered within, but she stopped partway down the corridor and entered a smaller room.

"Good evening," Fergus greeted her. "Glad you made it."

"Of course," Molly said, setting down her case. She took off her coat and hung it on a half-full rack. Then, smiling hello at the other members, including Mayor Tavish Calhoun and Officer Greer Anderson, she kicked off her boots and put on the gillies. "I even had a chance to practice a little this afternoon."

"Good for you, lass," Alastair said. "You've really improved since you started."

"I'm so glad you think so. Some days I don't feel like that, so it means a lot coming from you," Molly told him honestly.

While the bagpipers all took out their instruments and began to tune up, Molly caught Greer's eye and approached the officer. "We had an interesting experience last night at Neeps and Tatties."

"You did?" Greer asked with a frown. "We didn't get a call about it."

"You wouldn't have," Molly said, unlatching her case. "It was more strange than criminal." The problem with the incident, she realized, was that no crime had been committed. The restaurant was a public place and the front door, at least, had been unlocked at the time. Its significance lay in the covert nature of the intruder's behavior.

"Now I'm really intrigued." Greer glanced at Alastair, who was trying to herd the pipers into a semblance of a line. "Hurry. We don't have much time."

Molly filled the officer in while both made their way to the rear of the line. Along the way, Molly checked her instrument to be sure everything was okay, then cradled it in her arms. She'd already tuned up at home.

"That is strange," Greer said in a whisper as they began to march out of the room. "But maybe it was someone who had been at the party. They could have forgotten something and come back for it without making a show of it."

Molly weighed that possibility. The weather had been bad, and whoever it was might have been in a hurry to get home after collecting their phone or wallet. They might have left without saying anything. However, there was one thing the officer hadn't factored in. "You could be right, but then why didn't Fergus and Brodie see the person? He or she should have still been in the parking lot."

Greer shrugged. "We'll have to talk about that later." Fixing her gaze ahead, she lifted the mouthpiece to her lips, waiting for Alastair's signal.

The group of pipers marched out to the main room, where they formed a sharper line. At Alastair's signal, they launched into "My Heart's in the Highlands," and Molly forced herself to concentrate on the song and nothing else. Next, they played while The Leaping Lowlanders performed two Scottish country dances.

After the dancing ended, followed by much applause, Grizela addressed the crowd. "Wasn't that a lovely performance by our own Piping Yoopers and Leaping Lowlanders? After dinner, we're going to do some more dancing—and this time we hope all of you will participate." She scanned the crowd. "I'm glad to see many of you have gotten into the spirit of our Burns Week. And didn't our decorators do a lovely job?"

Now that the stress of performing was over for the moment, Molly could relax enough to study the room. Most of the guests, including Grizela, were dressed in Scottish garb or costumes reminiscent of the 1700s. Molly spotted the three out-of-town fishermen from the tournament, and even they were wearing tartan jackets. Small lanterns on the white-clothed tables, swags of plaid draped on the wall, and a few well-placed suits of armor gave the usually utilitarian room the feeling of a Highland ballroom. Place settings of hand-painted glass goblets, rustic pottery dinnerware, and plaid napkins continued the theme.

"In a minute we're going to open the buffet line," Grizela went on. "We've got a wonderful array of dishes to sample tonight, and a selection of hot and cold drinks that our volunteer servers will be bringing around." She gestured toward a group of men and women wearing aprons. Molly recognized Noah and Tara Taggart first, then spotted Brodie and Catriona standing at the back.

Molly was glad to see that the McCauleys felt comfortable enough to participate in a public event. She noticed Greer glancing their way and wondered what was going through the young officer's mind. Hopefully the police were continuing to investigate instead of considering the case closed.

Carol and Laura had saved seats at their table, so Molly and Fergus joined them after putting away their instruments. "That was great," Laura said to Molly. "Bagpipe music always gives me chills."

"My playing would give anyone chills," Molly joked.

"Hush," Carol said. "You were wonderful. Wasn't she, Harvey?"

Harvey, who was chatting with Sheldon Barker about fishing, took a moment to register the question. "Huh? Yes, that's right. Good job, Molly. You too, Fergus." He gave them two thumbs-up.

"I wonder what's on the menu tonight," Fergus said. "I have to admit I'm starving." Dishes of vegetables had been set on the tables, and he selected a piece of celery, then dunked it in a creamy dip.

"Me too," Molly said. "I eat so much more in cold weather, it seems." She took a carrot stick, hoping that would take the edge off her hunger.

Brodie arrived with a pitcher. "Mulled cider? It's really good, made from a wonderful new recipe Catriona discovered."

"What's in it?" Sheila asked, her usual sour expression on display. "I'm allergic to certain things."

Seated beside her, Sheldon shifted in his seat. He opened his mouth briefly but didn't say anything. Instead, he began to play with his silverware while casting frequent glances around the room.

Brodie rattled off the ingredients, "Apple cider, cranberry juice, orange peel, cloves, cinnamon sticks, ginger, and honey."

"All right," Sheila said, pursing her lips suspiciously. "I'll try it."

"I'd love some," Carol said brightly, as if to counteract Sheila's lack of enthusiasm. "Mulled cider is perfect on a cold night, don't you think?"

Everyone else also wanted cider, so Brodie went around the table filling the goblets, then hurried away to refill the empty pitcher.

Harvey clinked his goblet with Sheldon's. "Hope you can make it out to the loch tomorrow," he said. "The hometown team needs you."

As the two men began to talk about fishing again, Sheila gave a little huff and turned to Carol. "Do you ever feature local artists in the bakehouse? I'd love to display my paintings there."

"We haven't so far," Carol said, and Molly could hear the discomfort in her voice. They were likely both recalling the abstract Burns portrait Sheila had painted, which wasn't exactly the bakehouse's style. "Right now we're pretty happy with our—"

"I think they called this table," Laura said as she stood. "Let's go."

They all rose, chairs scraping, and made their way to the buffet table.

"Saved by the dinner bell," Carol whispered to Molly as they got in line. "I hate to say no to anyone, but . . ."

"Her art doesn't exactly fit our Scottish Northwoods vibe," Molly finished. "I get it." She took a plate off the pile and filled it with Finnan haddie—another name for cold-smoked haddock—along with peas, garlic mashed potatoes, and a soft roll that was still warm.

After dinner was over, Molly and the other Piping Yoopers retrieved their bagpipes. An area had been cleared for dancing, and guests started forming sets of couples. Laura was asked to dance by the burly fisherman named Sam. Soon the hall rang with rollicking Highland music and the thumping of feet as people marched, spun, and hopped.

Then, in the brief pause between songs, a scream rang out. "Somebody help me! Something's wrong with my husband!"

Sheila Barker was leaning over Sheldon, who lay writhing on the floor.

11

The scene in the community room dissolved into chaos. Someone called 911, and those who knew medical procedures raced to Sheldon's side to try to help.

"Everyone stand back," Fergus commanded, urging curious onlookers to give the volunteers room.

Molly set down her bagpipes and joined the crowd. Carol had her arm around Sheila, who was hunched over in anguish.

"We were watching the music when he fell off his chair," Sheila choked out. She gestured toward the goblets on the table. "Right after he drank some mulled cider."

A thrill of alarm ran through Molly. Maybe Sheldon wasn't merely ill. He might have been poisoned. She pointed to the cups. "Which one did he drink from?"

"Mine," Sheila said, then gasped, her hand flying to her mouth. Apparently Molly's suspicion had occurred to her.

"Are you sure?" Molly asked. "How do you know?"

"He finished his with dinner and that waiter hadn't come back, so he was drinking mine. I didn't like it, so I only had a sip."

Molly bit her lip and surreptitiously waved to Greer.

Greer frowned but made her way to Molly's side. "What is it?"

Molly drew Greer aside, out of earshot of others, and showed her the half-full goblet. "Sheila said he fell ill after drinking from her cup."

The officer folded her arms. "Maybe it was a coincidence. It looks to me as if he's having heart problems or suffering from food poisoning. Hard to tell until he gets to the hospital."

Food poisoning didn't preclude poison. In fact it could be another indication of it.

"Please," Molly implored. "Do me a favor and secure these cups and their contents. Once they're washed, the evidence will be gone."

"Evidence of what?" Greer wanted to know. But then she shook her head with a sigh. "No, don't tell me. I don't want you swaying my investigation. There's no harm in being cautious, I suppose." She found her cell phone and placed a call. "I called the chief," she reported to Molly after she hung up, her face set in grim lines. "He agrees with us getting involved. After what happened the other night . . ."

Molly filled in the words Greer didn't say. With a recent murder, they had to be extra vigilant when it came to other incidents. She noticed Brodie and Catriona standing together on the fringe of the crowd. Was Brodie going to be blamed for Sheldon's illness as well? Her heart sank. Probably so, since he had been serving the cider that Catriona had made.

The paramedics arrived swiftly, followed by Officer Murdoch and Chief Thomson. Greer shooed Molly away from the table, but she watched as Office Murdoch gathered the goblets and their contents. Then Chief Thomson took Brodie and Catriona aside and questioned them briefly before they went into the kitchen, where no doubt the chief was checking out the pot of mulled cider.

"What's going on?" Bridget appeared at Molly's side, still wearing her Leaping Lowlanders costume—a white, lace-necked blouse, a black vest, and a traditional plaid kilt.

"I'm not sure," Molly said, eyeing the stricken insurance agent, who now appeared to be unconscious. "But it's not looking good."

"Poor man," Bridget said, clasping her hands in distress. "I think I've served him at the bakehouse."

"He and his wife moved to town recently, so you probably did." Molly hadn't seen him, so he must have come in while she wasn't there.

With great efficiency and little fanfare, the medical workers loaded Sheldon onto a gurney for transport to the hospital. Sheila grabbed their coats and her handbag, ready to accompany her husband.

"Want us to drive you to the hospital, Sheila?" Carol asked. She gestured to Harvey to join her. "Unless you want to ride in the ambulance."

Sheila's face sagged with relief. "Would you? That's so kind."

After Harvey and Carol left with Sheila, Chief Thomson and Officer Murdoch right behind them, The Piping Yoopers returned to their performance. It took a few minutes, but soon the festive atmosphere returned. Laura partnered with Sam again and was having a great time dancing.

But Molly couldn't shake off her dire thoughts no matter how hard she tried to focus on playing. Until they had a medical diagnosis, she reminded herself, nothing much more could be done. Maybe they would learn that Sheldon had a bad reaction to food or had been stricken with a medical condition, as Greer thought . . . which would beg the question, why had his wife so quickly jumped to the conclusion of foul play? And the fact that he had sipped from her goblet made it all even stranger. Why would anyone attempt to hurt Sheila? Molly resolved to find out why Sheila believed that someone had tried. *Of course, she could just be worried because Finlay was killed a few days ago,* Molly reminded herself. *Sometimes murder is contagious.*

Over by the door, Catriona and Brodie slipped on coats and boots. Both of them appeared upset, and no wonder. Was the finger of suspicion going to be pointed at Brodie again?

By the time the performance ended, they still hadn't heard from Carol, so Molly and Laura decided to drive over to the Kinnaird Medical Center and offer support.

"You seemed to have fun dancing tonight," Molly observed, eager to talk about something besides Sheldon for a minute.

Laura beamed. "I sure did. Sam is quite a good dancer for such a big guy." She slowed as they approached a stop sign. "He and his friends are from Marquette. They're all heavy machine operators."

"Really?" It seemed like everyone Molly was meeting lately was from Marquette. "Did he have anything interesting to say?"

Laura shrugged. "We didn't talk much because we were dancing and the music was loud. But he did mention knowing Sheldon and Sheila. Sam gets his insurance from another firm Sheldon used to work for."

"Small world. He didn't go to Finlay's college, did he?" Molly asked. Not only were the visitors and new residents from the same city, they seemed to all know each other. But maybe that wasn't so surprising. After all, many people discovered Loch Mallaig via word of mouth.

"If so, he didn't say," Laura said. "But I do know he wanted to ask me out. It took some fancy stepping to avoid that politely, I can tell you." She smiled wryly. "He's nice but not quite my type."

"And what sort of guy is your type?" Molly asked in a teasing tone. Laura dated frequently but she hadn't been in a serious relationship for years.

"I'll know him when I see him," she said. "In the meantime, I'm quite happy with my friends, family, and work."

Kinnaird Medical Center was less than a mile from downtown, and soon they were pulling into the emergency room entrance. Carol's car was parked in a visitor's space near the door.

"They're still here," Molly said, gripped with both hope and dread. She and Laura grabbed their purses and hurried inside.

With a swish of the big doors, Molly and Laura entered the emergency room, which was quiet at this time of night. Besides the attendant at the desk, Carol and Harvey were the only two people there. The couple sat in a corner, watching a silent television set to the weather channel.

Carol jumped up when she saw them. "You came." Then, anticipating their question, she shook her head as she sank back down. "No news yet. Sheila is in the room with Sheldon and the doctor."

Molly unzipped her coat and perched on a chair beside Carol while Laura sat on the other side next to Harvey. "Do they know what's wrong?" Molly asked.

Carol pressed her lips together. "It wasn't a heart attack. Likely something he ingested."

More evidence of poison. But who had given it to him? The same person who had killed Finlay? Almost everyone who had attended the first Burns supper was also at the community center that evening. But different methods had been used—an arrow for Finlay and possibly poison on Sheldon. A Burns poem mentioned death by arrow. Did one mention poison? Molly couldn't remember. She picked up her phone and began to search the Internet.

"What are you looking for?" Carol asked.

"I have a theory that might be crazy. Robert Burns wrote a poem that mentioned an arrow. I'm wondering if he had another one to fit this situation." She found it quickly. "Listen to this, 'Toads with their poison, doctors with their drug.'"

"What does that mean?" Laura asked, puzzled. "I don't get it."

"I think whoever is trying to hurt people was inspired by Burns's poems. Poetic justice of sorts?" Even as Molly said the words, she knew how outlandish the notion sounded. But her theory also made an odd sort of sense.

Laura's eyes widened. "Do you really think . . ." She pulled out her phone and began to scroll. "I had no idea that Robert Burns wrote so many epitaphs. I hope someone else won't be next."

Cold snaked down Molly's spine at the thought of additional deaths. When would this end? *Not until we have the killer.*

The door to the patient area opened and Sheila emerged, ushered forward by a doctor. She was crying, one hand pressed to her mouth. Molly and her friends straightened, guessing the bad news.

"Sheldon's gone," Sheila said between sobs. "They couldn't save him."

Molly leaped to her feet, followed by her friends. "Oh, Sheila. I'm so sorry." She gathered the woman into a hug, then handed her clean tissues from a box set on a table nearby.

"Do you know what happened to him?" Harvey asked the doctor, his kind face creased with dismay. "It was so sudden."

The doctor shook his head. "We're not certain yet. We'll be running some tests." He said a few quiet words to the distraught widow, then excused himself. Judging by the doctor's bowed head and shoulders as he returned to the patient area, Molly guessed that the loss was weighing heavily upon him.

Sheila mopped at her eyes with a tissue. "I don't even know what to do next." She sniffed, glancing around the empty room. "How am I going to get home?"

"We'll take you," Carol said. "Is there anyone who can stay with you?"

Before Sheila could answer, the entrance doors swished open and Jeanne Dupont entered, hair loose and tangled, her coat buttoned incorrectly. She'd obviously rushed to the hospital.

"I just heard," Jeanne hurried over to Sheila and put a hand on her arm. "How is he?"

Sheila's answer was a headshake.

"Oh no!" Jeanne cried as she wrapped her arms around Sheila. "You poor thing. Come with me. I'll take you home. Or you can stay at the resort with me. Your choice."

"The resort sounds nice," Sheila said. "I'm not ready to go to the house yet." She pulled away from Jeanne. "Let me get my coat and bag."

Molly was relieved. She and her friends could go home knowing that the new widow was in good hands.

Sheila shrugged into her coat and picked up her purse, her movements stiff and slow. She fished around inside the handbag, searching for something. Then, holding out a piece of paper, she turned to face the others. "Do you think this had something to do with Sheldon's death?" Her hand shook. "It came in the mail today, in an envelope addressed to me."

Molly peered at the paper, not wanting to touch it. She nearly recoiled as she read aloud, "'Cut it out or you're next.'"

"That sounds like a threat to me," Harvey said, breaking the chilled silence that had fallen over the small group.

"Have you told the police about that note?" Laura asked.

Sheila shook her head. "Not yet." Her eyes were frightened. "I was trying to get up the nerve to tell Sheldon. You see, I think it had something to do with . . ." Her voice trailed off. "That doesn't matter now. I thought maybe after I showed him the note, we could go to the station together." Her face crumpled. "But we never made it. And after he got sick, I was too confused and upset to think. And the police were *right there.*"

"That's totally understandable," Jeanne said with a rueful smile, patting Sheila on the shoulder. "I was a complete mess when I found out about Finlay. Still am."

Molly pulled out her phone. "I'm calling the chief. He needs to see that note right away." She dialed 911, and the dispatcher put her right through.

"Chief," she said, "this is Molly Ferris. I'm at the hospital with Sheila Barker. There's bad news about Sheldon." She swallowed, blinking back sudden tears. "He didn't make it."

"I'm very sorry to hear that," Chief Thomson said. "But why are *you* informing me of this?"

Molly took a few steps away and turned her back. "I'm sure you'll be hearing from the doctor. They're not sure what killed him." She dragged in a deep breath. "But there's more. Sheila got a threatening note earlier today. She just showed it to us."

"What?" The chief's roared response was so loud Molly had to hold the phone away from her ear. "Stay there. I'll come right over." He disconnected.

"He'll be here soon," she said to the others. "So if you don't mind waiting . . ."

Jeanne plopped onto a chair. "Of course not. The sooner they get to the bottom of the situation, the better." A series of emotions drifted across her face, as if understanding was dawning. "Do you think the two deaths are connected? Finlay and Sheldon?"

Sheila sat beside her. "I think they must be." Her eyes narrowed. "Especially since Brodie McCauley served us tonight."

12

Hot denials about Brodie's guilt rushed to Molly's lips and Laura let out a yelp. Harvey stepped forward as though to say something, but Carol put a restraining hand on his arm, then glanced at her friends with raised eyebrows.

Molly inhaled deeply, knowing now was not the time or place to defend Brodie or argue with Sheila. She needed to remain calm and collected and learn all she could. But then she thought of a question she needed to ask. "Sheila, Brodie didn't have any quarrel with Sheldon, did he? Or you?" To her relief, her tone was sufficiently neutral, not revealing how anxious she was to hear the answer.

Sheila's smile was triumphant. "Oh yes, he certainly did. We had lots of problems with Brodie." She clicked her tongue. "Talk about a difficult customer. The claim he filed wasn't being settled nearly fast enough for him. He was quite angry about it."

Molly was about to answer that red tape was rarely a motive for murder, and that Brodie was unlikely to kill the only person who could speed the process along for him, but she saw a Loch Mallaig cruiser pull up outside the big lobby windows. A moment later, the chief and Officer Murdoch climbed out and headed toward the hospital entrance. There was one point she wanted to make with the chief tonight, and she'd better do it quickly, before he became embroiled with Sheila and the hospital staff.

She hurried out to the vestibule to greet the officers. "Chief, Officer Murdoch. Thanks for getting here so quickly." Then her words dried up and she stood blocking their way, shifting from foot to foot.

"What is it, Molly?" Chief Thomson asked in a patient tone. But Molly sensed she shouldn't try that patience much longer.

"I've been doing some research," she said quickly. "And both methods of death are from Robert Burns poems. Either that, or we have an amazing coincidence on our hands. Read 'Second Epistle to Robert Graham' and 'A Mother's Lament.'"

Both officers stared at her with bewildered expressions. "All right," the chief said after a moment. "I'll take that under advisement. Did you get the names of those poems, Murdoch?"

"What were they again, Mrs. Ferris?" the officer asked.

She repeated the poem names slowly. "If you don't remember, you can search for 'arrow' and 'poison' and 'Robert Burns poems.' That's how we found them."

While Officer Murdoch made a note, the chief asked, "Anything else?"

As Molly glanced toward the lobby, where everyone was waiting for the officers, she realized there was another piece of information she wanted to share. "Remember our conversation about the people who knew Finlay Croft?" He nodded, and she went on. "They were all at the community center tonight, except for Jeanne Dupont. She probably wasn't feeling especially festive."

"I can understand that," the chief said. "Now, if that's all, Molly, we'd better get to work."

Molly stepped aside to let the officers pass, hoping against hope that what she had shared would help solve the mystery of not one death, but two.

"I wonder if they'll find anything at Sheila's house," Molly said to Laura as they drove back to town a short while later. The chief had gently suggested that everyone but Sheila leave the hospital. They were taking the threatening letter very seriously, and Molly had gathered they headed out to the Barker home immediately. Afterward, the officers would drop Sheila off at the resort to stay with Jeanne.

"Hopefully they will," Laura said. "She said she threw away the envelope, but I assume they'll search the trash."

"I don't get it," Molly said. "You'd think that someone would blame the insurance agent if there was a problem, not the office clerk."

Laura slowed to turn into the bakehouse driveway. "Maybe she's hard to deal with."

"I can see that," Molly said. "She's a difficult personality. Even her husband admitted it." Molly felt a pang. Her *dead* husband. Poor Sheila. After Laura halted the car, Molly opened the door. "Want to come up for a hot drink before heading home?"

"I'd love to." Laura put the car into park and switched off the engine. "I'm tired and also on edge. Certainly not quite ready for bed."

Upstairs, Laura gave Angus attention while Molly put on milk for hot cocoa. She found some peppermint marshmallows in the cupboard leftover from Christmas. They were still soft, so she used them to top the cocoa.

They sat at the kitchen table to sip the comforting drink. Angus crunched a biscuit as he cuddled up to Molly's feet.

"I have an idea," Laura said, checking the weather on her phone. "Tomorrow's Sunday, so the bakehouse will be closed. Why don't you, Carol, and I take a road trip to Marquette? It's supposed to be sunny and almost warm."

"To investigate?" Molly asked, knowing the answer. All the players involved in the two deaths came from Marquette. Maybe they could uncover some answers or connections there.

"You bet." Laura's smile was sly. "And go shopping. I heard that retail therapy helps cure bad cases of cabin fever."

Molly laughed. "Bring it on, then." She thought of the little Scottie under the table. "Since we'll be gone all day, I'll ask Bridget to stop by and take Angus for walks." The thump of his short tail against her foot told her he approved of this plan.

"Sounds good to me." Laura sipped her cocoa. "Why don't we go to early church and leave right after the service?"

That would bring them to Marquette around noon. "Sure. We can eat a quick lunch when we get there and then make our rounds." She brought up a map on her phone and located Barrie-Firth College, which was conveniently near the best shopping and some restaurants. She rattled off a few names to Laura. "Any of these sound good?"

"Hmm." Laura's eyes lit up. "I know a great place to stop for a meal. At my parents' house."

"That's right, they live in Marquette," Molly said with a smile. Her own parents lived in Iowa, and she didn't blame Laura for wanting to see hers when she had the chance. Even in their fifties, it was nice to get a home-cooked meal once in a while. "It's a plan."

Molly, Carol, and Laura were on the road by ten the next morning in Carol's comfortable Chrysler, Laura in front and Molly in back with a picnic basket. After Laura spoke to her parents, they'd decided to eat lunch on the way and then swing by the Donovan house later for dinner. Marie Donovan had promised to make her famous chicken and dumplings, one of Laura's favorite childhood meals.

This time of year, traffic on the highway was sparse and they zipped along, alone on the road for long stretches. Carol had tuned the radio to a pleasant easy-listening station and Molly sat back in the comfortable seat and tried to relax.

So much had happened over the past few days. She allowed her mind to roam over the incidents, starting with Finlay Croft assuming the orator role. Or had things started when he was judging the fishing contest? Whichever it was, his presence in Loch Mallaig had proven to be a disruptive force.

"Have either of you heard anything more about last night?" Molly asked.

They shook their heads. Carol turned the radio down. "I've been wondering if they found any other evidence at the Barkers' home."

Molly pulled out her phone. "I'll text Jeanne and ask. She's probably up to date since Sheila is staying with her."

Within a couple of minutes, her phone rang. Molly stared at it in surprise when Jeanne's name appeared on the screen. She'd expected a text, not a call. "Jeanne? We're traveling so I might lose you."

"Oh, where are you going?" Jeanne asked.

"We're doing a little shopping out of town," Molly answered, intentionally making her response vague. "How are you?" She wanted to cut to the chase, but politeness trumped her eagerness.

Jeanne sighed. "I'm okay. I finally got Sheila to go up to the spa. The poor thing needs to relax. She's had a terrible loss, and she's not an easy person at the best of times."

"I hear you," Molly said. "Do you know if they found anything else at the house last night?"

Something rattled in the background, followed by the sound of pouring liquid. "Hold on, I'm getting a cup of coffee." The clank of a spoon stirring followed. "Okay, I'm back." She sipped loudly. "Apparently Officer Murdoch dug through the trash and found the envelope. But as Sheila had said, there wasn't a return address. It was one of the blank envelopes they send out with insurance premium bills."

"So it could have come from any of their clients," Molly said. Of course there wasn't a return address. What bad guy worth their salt would include one?

"Yes, I suppose so. And there wasn't a postmark. Someone put it in the box themselves."

"Interesting," Molly said. Very few people lived out near the Barkers, and she supposed the police would question neighbors to try and identify who had delivered the threat. "Anything else going on?"

"I did hear something," Jeanne said. "They're questioning Brodie McCauley again. Like Sheila said, he'd had conflicts with the Barkers."

Molly groaned. Poor Brodie. His bail would be revoked if he was charged with a second murder.

After Molly hung up, she shared what she'd learned with the others.

"We're not making this trip too soon," Carol said. "I hope we find some answers today."

"Me too," Laura put in, her voice forlorn. "Right now it's all too confusing."

Soon they were approaching the outskirts of Marquette. Located on the shores of Lake Superior and surrounded by national parks and forests, it was the largest city in the Upper Peninsula, although the population barely topped 20,000.

Traffic grew denser as they made their way onto the secondary streets. Carol had loaded Barrie-Firth College's address into her navigation, and the robotic voice called out directions. Soon they were approaching the small college, which featured a broad lawn surrounded by stately brick buildings.

"Now for the difficult part," Carol said. "Finding a parking space."

She circled the snow-covered green a couple of times until they spotted someone backing out. She waited, then quickly wheeled into the spot.

Molly fed quarters into the parking meter.

"The library is that way," Laura said, pointing across the green. Although she hadn't attended the school, she was familiar with the college's layout as a Marquette native. "It should be open. I'm sure students do a lot of their studying on the weekend."

Taking one of the cleared paths that cut across the green, the women hurried toward a modern brick building featuring a short tower and tall, mirrored windows. There they hoped to dig into college records and documents to learn more about Finlay Croft, Jeanne Dupont, and the Taggarts.

Bundled-up students passed them going both ways, heads down and expressions intent. Despite the frigid air and heaps of snow, the campus still had an air of energetic activity. Laura opened the library door, and they entered a vestibule. Straight ahead was an elevator, with doors leading to study rooms on one side and archives on the other. Grand staircases wound up to the second and main floor.

Just coming off a long drive, they naturally gravitated to the stairs and the chance to stretch their legs. At the top, they paused to unzip their coats, then passed through the security barriers into the quiet but busy space. Computer stations were set up in lines, long tables held students studying, and straight ahead was a reception desk.

Molly's gaze fell on a rack of student newspapers near the desk. *RIP Professor Finlay,* the headline read. Drawn as if by a magnet, she went to grab one off the pile.

A librarian behind the desk glanced up from her computer monitor. "It was quite a shock to the community," she said, with a nod at the paper. Middle-aged and comfortably plump, the librarian had a round, pleasant face and a head of dark curls. Her name tag read *Coretta Lee.*

Molly approached the desk, flanked by Laura and Carol. "Actually, we're from Loch Mallaig, where this happened." She gestured with the newspaper.

Coretta's mouth dropped open. "Really? What brings you to Marquette?"

"My parents live here," Laura said. "And we wanted to take a peek at your Scottish collection." Browsing the library's notable selection of rare editions by Robert Louis Stevenson, Arthur Conan Doyle and, of course, Robert Burns, was also on their to-do list, a golden opportunity they couldn't pass up.

The librarian nodded. "Many people visit us for that." She pointed to a side room. "It's in there when you're ready." Resting her hands on the counter, she dropped her voice. "What's the word up your way?"

Satisfaction glowed in Molly's chest. They couldn't ask for a better source than a curious librarian. "The police are investigating," she said. "One arrest has been made, but people are having a hard time accepting that the man is guilty."

Coretta's eyes flared with interest. "I heard about that on the news. Who do you think did it, if not the restaurant owner?"

"We have no idea," Carol said. "Do you?"

The librarian glanced both ways, then leaned closer and lowered her voice. "Professor Finlay wasn't exactly popular around here. He could be very demanding." She waved her hand at a stack of books. "Those, for example. Ordered through interlibrary loan from all over the country. Took forever, and he was breathing down my neck about it every step of the way."

"He won't be needing them now," Laura said wryly. "We heard that he fired his assistant?"

Coretta flashed a shrewd smirk. "Which one? He fired every single one of them. And maybe that wouldn't be a big deal, except the college has excellent benefits—great vacation, insurance, free tuition for dependents. Losing a job here can really hurt a person."

But only one ex-assistant was now in Loch Mallaig, as far as Molly knew—and that woman's son had lost out on free tuition. Thinking of Noah, she asked, "What about students? Was he popular with them?"

Coretta thought for a moment. "Most of the time, yes, actually. He was a good teacher, very passionate about Scottish literature. His enthusiasm was contagious with his students. But there was a scandal with one young man." Her expression sobered. "He was so promising. Everyone talked about his potential and how they expected great things from him. But there were rumors of cheating."

"Was he expelled?" Carol asked.

"No, he dropped out," Coretta said. "I often wonder what happened to him."

Molly guessed she was talking about Noah Taggart. Had he cheated? Or had he been wrongly accused? It sounded like nothing had been definitively proven, though he'd likely had to drop out after Tara lost her job. After a moment, when it became clear that Coretta had nothing more to tell them, Molly smiled. "Thanks for your help, Coretta. We're going to take a look at the Scottish collection."

"If you need anything, give a holler," Coretta said. "Well, not literally. This is a library, after all." With a laugh, she turned back to her computer.

The Bakehouse Three strolled across the library toward the Scottish room. Halfway there, Molly paused, noticing a public computer station. "We could do some digging online," she suggested.

"And I have another idea." Laura stopped a student walking by. "Where can I find back issues of the college newspaper?"

The young woman pointed to a rack of magazines. "We keep

old copies over there on the bottom shelves, along with copies of the special quarterly."

Laura smiled brightly. "Thanks."

"Great idea," Carol said after the student walked away. "We can leaf through those and see if anything jumps out at us."

"At the least we'll learn more background information." Laura led the way to the shelves. "Let's look there first, and then reward ourselves with the Scottish room."

"Sounds like a plan," Molly said, picking out college magazines from the previous year as well as current issues.

They carried their selections to a nearby table and spread out. They worked in silence, scanning the publications for mention of Finlay, Noah, Tara, or Jeanne.

"Hey," Laura whispered. "I found something." She angled a newspaper to show them. A large photograph at the bottom of the page showed the green in spring, with people lounging, sitting on benches, and throwing Frisbees. Daffodils bloomed in flower beds.

"What are we looking at?" Carol asked, squinting at the page.

Laura stabbed her finger at the paper, landing on a couple sitting on a bench. "That's Sheldon Barker and Tara Taggart. How do they know each other?"

"I don't know," Molly said as she and Carol leaned over to peer at the photograph. It was grainy, even for black and white, but one thing was clear to Molly. "Is it just me, or does it look like they were extremely close?"

13

Speculations whirled in Molly's mind. Had it been coincidence, a simple sharing of a seat in the sun? But Sheldon was angled toward Tara, his mouth open as if he was saying something to her, although she was staring straight ahead.

Maybe she was an insurance client? But surely that type of meeting would take place in Sheldon's office. The only thing they really knew was that Tara and Sheldon were acquainted and now Sheldon was dead.

A truly wild thought darted into Molly's mind. Perhaps Tara had convinced Sheldon to kill Finlay, her hated ex-boss. And then she had killed him to cover her tracks.

She snorted at herself. *Talk about a far-fetched scenario.*

Laura's eyes met hers. She patted the page. "This could mean nothing—or everything. We need to talk to Tara."

"Agreed," Carol said. "We were already aware that Tara worked for Finlay. But I had no idea she also knew Sheldon."

"I wonder if she knows Sheila," Molly mused. But what motive would Tara have to kill Sheila? To get her out of the way of a romance with Sheldon? She shuddered. If so, that bloodthirsty move had certainly backfired.

Laura took a picture of the photograph with her phone. "We'll go ask her after we get back to town."

"Should we keep this up?" Carol asked, waving a hand at the pile of newspapers in front of her seat. "Or are we done here?"

Molly glanced at her pile. "I only have one more magazine to flip through. Why don't we keep going for a few more minutes?"

"Sure," Laura said, setting her phone down. "I haven't found much on Finlay. Just a couple of articles about his department, and they were pretty tame. No controversy or anything."

Molly began leafing through the glossy magazine. This issue was focused on sports at Barrie-Firth, with articles about the teams and college history. Tennis, basketball, swimming... and archery. A picture of the team accompanied the write-up about archery, with student and coach names listed below. As one in particular sunk in, Molly issued a yelp of surprise, drawing her friends' attention.

She showed them the article. "Noah Taggart was on the archery team," she whispered.

Laura took the magazine and snapped another photo. "Motive, means, and opportunity. Noah had all three."

A few hours later, Carol pulled up in front of the Donovan home, a cream-colored foursquare flanked by large maples that must look fantastic in autumn. Steps from the sidewalk led up to the house, which was fronted with a wide, welcoming porch.

"Home sweet home," Laura said, a smile in her voice. She opened the car door in haste, obviously eager to see her parents.

Molly retrieved her purse from amid a pile of shopping bags and climbed out. Once they'd browsed the library's Scottish collection for a while, they had indulged in a shopping trip. The January sales were too good to resist, and Molly's wardrobe had received some much-needed upgrades.

Laura knocked twice before opening the door. She stepped into the foyer and called out, "Mom? Dad? I'm home."

Kirk Donovan appeared in the doorway to the left, a folded

newspaper in his hand. "There's my girl." Lean and wiry, Kirk had silvery hair and twinkling eyes. He hugged his daughter, then eyed Molly and Laura. Having been friends with Laura since college, they had known the Donovans for more than thirty years. "And you brought the cavalry, I see."

As Carol and Molly greeted Kirk, Marie Donovan came bustling from the rear of the house, wiping her hands on her apron. "Hello, favorite daughter," she sang out, then pulled Laura into a tight embrace.

Laura laughed as she returned the hug. "I'm your *only* daughter."

Marie smiled. "Well, you and your brother were always concerned with which of you was the favorite." She enthusiastically hugged Carol, then Molly. "It's wonderful to see you again. Did you have a good drive down?"

They chatted about the roads and the weather as Marie ushered them into the living room and settled them into comfortable chairs. Dinner was almost ready, the table set in the adjacent dining room, and Marie refused any help.

"You might as well relax," Kirk said with a fond smile. "You know how your mother is. The hostess with the mostest."

"I do know," Laura agreed.

"You certainly take after her," Carol said to Laura. "The bakehouse wouldn't be the same without you." She smiled at Kirk. "Your daughter bakes the most incredible breads and treats. We're developing a huge fan base."

Kirk beamed with pride. "That's my Laura. She's been baking ever since we got her that little light-bulb oven."

Laura scoffed. "I think I baked one cake in there before I started bugging Mom about using the real oven."

Sitting back with a sigh, Molly listened to the others chat. It was so relaxing to bask in warmth from the crackling fireplace, listening to light conversation between people she'd known for decades. Kirk had the television on, but the sound had been muted.

Then words scrolled across the bottom of the screen that clenched her stomach in cold fingers: *Murder in Loch Mallaig.*

Carol noticed it too. "Can you please turn that up?" she asked Laura's father.

The group watched the feature, glued to the update about the two deaths in Loch Mallaig. A brief recap of Finlay's murder was followed by news of Sheldon's mysterious death. Brodie had been taken in for questioning, the reporter said, but no further charges had been filed yet.

After the story was over, Kirk switched the sound off again. "You know what struck me about the professor's murder? Whoever did that must have been quite a crack shot. It's not easy to use a bow and arrow at night without some kind of special equipment."

"Like what, Dad?" Laura asked.

"I have some friends who hunt," Kirk explained. "Believe it or not, night hunting is legal in Michigan. They like to challenge their skills that way, so they use special sights or lights."

"That's an interesting point," Laura said. "I wonder if the police found any night-hunting equipment at Brodie's house or at the restaurant."

"I haven't heard that they did," Carol said. "But of course they wouldn't necessarily share that information with the public."

Molly wondered how she could ask Chief Thomson without implying that he wasn't conducting the investigation properly. He was an excellent law enforcement officer, and she respected him greatly. At the very least, they could ask Brodie if he ever practiced archery after dark.

Marie came to the living room doorway. "Dinner's on the table," she announced. "As promised, we're having homemade chicken and dumplings tonight." With expressions of delight and hunger, everyone stood up and stretched.

At the table, conversation became general as Carol and Molly gave Mr. and Mrs. Donovan updates about the bakehouse and their own families. Laura shared the new recipes she'd been trying, to her mother's delight. Kirk didn't mention the murders, and Molly wondered if he was trying to avoid worrying his wife. They really were a charming couple—energetic, devoted to their family, and obviously still in love after more than fifty years together.

When the meal ended, the trio finally tore themselves away from the Donovans' comfortable home and headed back to Loch Mallaig. "All in all, a very good day," Carol said as they merged onto the highway. "We need to do this more often."

"Totally agree," Laura said. "My parents were so tickled to see us. I'm working on getting them to come for a visit, but they don't go far in the winter."

Molly, in the back seat again, studied the dark countryside as they sped along. Traffic was light and the roads clear, so they should make great time. She was so tempted to pass along the information they had gathered to the chief, but caution held her back. The last thing she wanted to do was ruin her good relationship with the department. Not that she tried to get herself involved in murder cases, but somehow it seemed to happen more than she'd like. She'd rather be perceived as being of help, not a hindrance or an annoyance.

Then she thought of something . . . well, *someone*. Trustworthy Fergus would never tell a soul anything she shared. She really liked that about him, especially since it was human nature to spill secrets. Without thinking about it too much, she dashed off a text giving him an update on what they had learned at the college. Then she mentioned Kirk's point about the probable use of night equipment.

Fergus must have still been awake because he wrote back immediately. *That's a very interesting detail. Brodie or Donal ought to be informed, as the night equipment angle could be critical to his defense. I'll stop by the bakehouse in the morning and we can chat about it more.*

Molly smiled, not sure which warmed her the most, his support in the investigation or the promise to come by the bakery. Either way, Fergus was becoming a fixture in her life—and she liked it very much.

To pass the time, she idly searched the Internet on her phone to see what night-hunting gear looked like. It seemed to feature sights or goggles with green lenses, apparently because human eyes are more sensitive to green light, so it helped them see better at night.

Finally, at half past ten, Carol pulled into the bakehouse drive, where Laura's car was parked. "Wow. A good day but a long one," Carol said with a yawn. "See you two in the morning."

"Thanks for driving," Molly said. "If you want to sleep in a little, feel free. I can handle setting up."

"I might take you up on that," Carol said. "Don't forget your bags."

Laura and Molly gathered their purchases and said good night. After Carol pulled away, Laura unlocked her car door. "I can't wait to get home. My pillow is calling my name."

Molly glanced across the street toward Neeps and Tatties. The lights were on, which meant that Brodie and Catriona were still there. "I was thinking about popping across the street to talk to the McCauleys."

"My pillow can wait." Laura tossed the bags into the passenger seat. "I'm going with you." She gestured to Molly. "Leave your bags here. You can get them when we come back."

Glad that her friend was joining her, Molly put her bags on the back seat. Then the pair walked across the street to the restaurant. The front door was locked, but Molly knocked on the glass.

"We're closed," Catriona called, crossing the carpet. Then she saw who was at the door and hurried to unlock it. "Oh, it's you! Please come in."

"We won't stay long," Molly promised. She unzipped her coat but didn't take it off. "We went to Marquette today and have some information we'd like to share with you and Brodie."

Catriona's eyes flared with interest. She gestured for them to follow. "Don't worry about your boots. We haven't vacuumed yet." The chef bustled across the room, pausing only to gesture for them to wait at the fireside, then pushed open the kitchen door. "Brodie?" she called. A shout answered her. He was somewhere in the depths of the building.

Molly and Laura stood near the fireplace, which still contained smoldering embers. A moment later, the couple came out of the kitchen, Catriona in the lead.

Brodie was wiping his hands on a rag. He had circles under his eyes, Molly noted with sympathy. "Sorry, I was cleaning the walk-in. How are you ladies tonight?"

Molly told him about their visit to the Barrie-Firth College library. "We learned a couple of things that you might want to pass along to your attorney. First, Noah Taggart was on the archery team." She winced a little after hearing her blunt statement and added hastily, "Not that I'm pointing fingers."

Catriona locked eyes with her husband. "I hate to think that Noah . . ." Her voice trailed off.

"I hate to think that anyone did such a thing—and in our parking lot to boot." Brodie's tone was dry. "Unfortunately there's no changing that it did happen. We need to keep an open mind, even if it means suspecting an employee." The distress in his expression belied his assertive words.

Molly had decided not to mention Tara and Sheldon sitting together on the bench. Right now that was pure gossip and didn't need to be dished just yet. Besides, they didn't even know what it might mean. However, there was more to share with the McCauleys. "There's another thing. Laura's father raised a good point."

The couple shifted focus to Laura, who cleared her throat. "Dad has a lot of friends who hunt. He said that to be accurate at night, the killer probably used some kind of special gear."

"Do you shoot at night, Brodie?" Molly asked, holding her breath for the answer.

Brodie shook his head, a crease forming between his brows. "No. I only go target shooting during the day." He tapped a bicep. "For exercise and to keep up my skills."

"He never even goes hunting," Catriona added eagerly. "Thank you so much for this information. We'll talk to Mr. McNab in the morning."

Her husband sighed. "When he accompanies me to the station for another round of questioning."

"So they're looking at you for Sheldon's death?" Molly asked. At the couple's glum nods, she placed a reassuring hand on Catriona's arm. "Don't lose heart yet. I have a feeling that there's a lot more to learn when it comes to Sheldon Barker's life. And not all of it is rosy."

14

The aroma of cinnamon greeted Molly's nose when she went down-stairs the next morning. She found Laura in the kitchen, standing near the oven with a pair of mitts on.

"Yum," Molly said. "What's baking?"

Laura peered into the oven, then opened the door. "Plum custard tarts topped with brown sugar and cinnamon." She pulled out the tray holding a dozen mini tarts and set it on the counter to cool. Then she grabbed a tart and put it on a plate for Molly. "Carol's helping in her grandkids' class this morning and won't be in until later, so you can be my tester."

Molly's mouth was already watering. "Are you sure?" At Laura's nod, Molly took the plate, then grabbed a clean fork. While waiting for the treat to cool slightly, she poured a mug of coffee.

"I thought you, Carol, and I could take a few to Tara Taggart today," Laura said. "Welcome her to the neighborhood."

Molly, who had a mouthful of hot coffee, swallowed hard. "Ask her some questions, you mean."

Busy arranging another batch of tarts, Laura gave a one-shouldered shrug. "That too. I have to admit I'm really, really curious after seeing that photo of her with Sheldon. It's another connection we need to probe."

Molly sat at the counter. "Maybe he messed up her insurance claim."

Laura snorted. "I'm guessing it was a little deeper than that. Did you see the way he was gazing at her?"

Judging the tart was cool enough, Molly cut into it with her fork. "Maybe you're reading into it."

"I don't think so," Laura said. "I'll show you the picture again later."

Molly took a bite of tart and allowed it to melt in her mouth, tasting flaky pastry and creamy custard offset by the tang of plum. "Oh my. This is fantastic, Laura."

"So good to hear." Laura danced a little as she arranged plums in the tart shells.

The back door opened and, a moment later, Bridget hurried into the kitchen from the hallway. "Brrr. Another cold one today." She unwound the scarf that had covered the lower half of her face. Then she raised her nose into the air as she shrugged out of her coat. "What's that smell?"

"Plum tart," Molly said. "Come have one."

"You don't have to ask me twice. I skipped breakfast." Bridget slipped on an apron, poured a coffee, and all but bounded to the counter to join Molly.

"Oh to be young again." Molly shook her head at this display of youthful energy so early in the morning.

Laura placed a tart on a plate and set it in front of Bridget. Molly handed her a fork. Both watched as the college student took a bite.

"Oh my." Bridget rolled her eyes. "Yum." She pointed a fork at Laura. "You are the *master*." She started to take a second bite then stopped, arranging the fork just so on the plate. Reaching into her pocket, she pulled out her phone and snapped a shot. Thumbs working busily, she said, "I'm posting this right now. All my friends will rush over here."

"Thanks," Laura said, smiling. Her cheeks had pinked at Bridget's praise.

"They love this place," Bridget said. "And you know college students. They're always starving."

Molly couldn't argue with that. When Chloe had been in college, she and her friends would eat Molly out of house and home.

"That guy having an attack during dinner at the community center was pretty awful the other night," Bridget said, putting down her phone and returning to her tart. She frowned. "And I can't believe people are blaming Brodie. It was all anyone could talk about yesterday at school."

"I'll bet," Molly said, not surprised that the murders were the subject of gossip. "But we don't believe he did it."

"I don't either," Bridget said stoutly. "I know tons of people who have worked there and they all love Brodie and Catriona." She jabbed her fork into her tart. "You know who I saw at a party recently? That guy who works at Neeps sometimes. Noah."

It wasn't surprising that Noah would hang around with other young adults. "I don't really know him," Molly said. "What's he like?"

Bridget tipped her head back and forth, clearly mulling it over. "Hmm. He's obviously smart. And funny. But he seems . . . angry at the world. It kind of leaks out sometimes."

Molly thought back to her encounter in the park. Repressed anger was the emotion she'd sensed from the running figure. "He had some trouble at Barrie-Firth," she said. Then she put a finger to her lips. "That needs to stay here."

"Got it," Bridget said. Molly didn't trust many college-age girls to keep such gossip to themselves, but if Bridget promised something, she meant it. The girl scooped up her last bite of tart. "Well, whatever happens, I hope he can put it behind him. He said he's going to start taking classes at Superior Bay next semester."

A fresh start at Bridget's school sounded like a good idea for the young man. But then Molly wondered, was starting over easier without the man who had presumably ruined Noah's life and his mother's?

Bridget and Molly got the bakehouse front room ready for opening while Laura continued to bake. Despite the bone-chilling temperatures this morning, cars began to pull into the parking lot at opening time.

"I guess nothing keeps them away," Bridget said as the entrance bell jingled and the first group hustled inside, grousing about the weather. "That's good for us."

They went into action, serving up hot drinks and plating delicious baked goods from the display case. The bakehouse soon hummed with conversation and laughter.

Every time the door opened, Molly found herself glancing up to see who was coming in. Finally she spotted the face she'd been waiting for—Fergus. His nose and cheeks were red but his smile was cheerful as he waved at Molly.

"Plum tart?" Molly offered when he drew closer to the counter. "You'd better hurry, they're going fast."

Fergus eyed the two lonely tarts remaining in the case. "I think I will. And my usual coffee."

Molly hurried to prepare his beverage while Bridget plated a tart.

"Headed out to the fishing derby today?" Molly asked as she handed over his coffee.

He made a face. "I sure am. I'm going to need warmers for my feet and hands. It is absolutely brutal outside. And almost always windy on the loch."

"You're really going above and beyond." Molly shivered at the idea of spending time outside today. Poor Angus was going to get a very short walk. "Maybe you can sit in Harvey's bob-house part of the time."

Fergus grinned. "How'd you guess my secret? I'm planning to make the rounds, visit for a while with each fisherman. I can't stick with anyone too long, or people will accuse me of favoritism."

"I have an idea," Bridget said, gesturing to a big bakery box. "Why don't you take a box of baked goods with you? Then they'll definitely let you in the door."

Fergus grinned. "That's a great idea, Bridget. Give me two dozen, your choice."

Bridget got to work, selecting scones, bannocks, and pastries from the case.

"Thanks, Fergus," Molly said as she rang up his purchases. She lowered her voice. "You didn't have to agree."

His eyes twinkled. "But I wanted to." Fergus glanced around at the busy room. "As you can see, Bread on Arrival has a very good reputation in Loch Mallaig. And you're going to make some cold fishermen very, very happy today."

Bridget closed the bakery box lid. "I'll keep this here until you leave, Fergus." She smiled at Molly. "Why don't you take a break? I can handle things by myself for a few minutes."

Molly's heart leaped at the idea of spending some time with Fergus. She glanced at the clock. "Carol should be here any minute. But holler if you need me." Molly quickly dispensed a fresh mug of coffee and went to join Fergus.

They sat at a small table near the fireplace, one of Molly's favorite spots, especially in the dead of winter. She waited while he took the first bites of tart, murmuring his appreciation.

She laughed at his obvious delight. "Bridget and I got to test those this morning. They are fabulous, aren't they?"

Fergus cut off another bite. "You're always surprising us with something new and delicious. Laura is amazing."

"She is," Molly agreed. "We had dinner with her parents last night. They are just the sweetest."

"In Marquette?" Fergus raised a brow. "What'd you do in the city?"

Molly took a sip of coffee, prolonging the suspense, then said, "We did a little research at the Barrie-Firth library."

"The college where Finlay Croft worked?"

"That's the one."

"Come on, don't leave me hanging. What did you find?"

Setting down her mug, Molly leaned forward. "We encountered a very chatty librarian, for one thing."

"Oh, the best kind," Fergus said.

She relayed what Coretta Lee had told them about Finlay, then shared about the photograph of Sheldon and Tara, and Noah's membership on the archery team. "Coretta made a point of telling us how promising Noah had been. She seemed to consider his dropping out to be quite a disappointment."

"What happened?" Fergus asked, taking the last bite of tart. He'd been riveted the whole time Molly had been speaking.

"Something about cheating, according to rumor. But Noah wasn't expelled or anything. He left the college."

Fergus's brows knit in thought. "But Finlay was involved?"

"I got the impression he was the one who raised the issue of cheating."

"Hmm." Fergus fiddled with his fork. "There are certainly dots to connect here. If Noah felt like Finlay ruined his life . . ."

"And his mother's." Molly's belly tightened with a mix of excitement and revulsion. The pieces were coming together. "Finlay fired her. And it appears that she knew Sheldon too."

Fergus put up a hand. "It's a reasonable theory, but only that. We'd better not fire off any accusations yet. A lot of people know how to use a bow and arrow around here."

Molly's nerves loosened. She wasn't quite ready to think that a college student was a killer. "You're right. We don't know enough."

She picked up her mug. "We're going to visit Tara later. Maybe we can learn a little more about her and her son."

Fergus appeared troubled. "Tara is doing a nice job at the resort. For her sake, I sincerely hope her son is innocent."

"I know this is a long shot, but do you happen to know her schedule today?"

"As a matter of fact, I reviewed the schedule last night," Fergus said. "Her shift starts at three this afternoon."

"Thanks for the info."

"Anytime." Fergus stood. "Now I'd best collect my pastries and head out once more unto the breach."

"Aren't you supposed to quote Burns instead of Shakespeare this week?" Molly asked with a laugh. "Either way, you'll be a hero with your arsenal of treats."

Fergus grinned. "Can't ask for better than that."

By tapping into the Loch Mallaig rumor mill, Molly learned that Tara was renting a house near the loch not far from Castleglen and Laura's cottage. Not wanting to disturb her at work, Molly, Laura, and Carol left Bridget and Hamish in charge at the bakehouse and headed over to visit Tara.

As they drove down the road, Laura pointed out a beautiful modern house. "That's the Barkers' place. I saw Sheila outside when I went for a run the other day."

"Interesting that the Barkers and Tara live so close to each other," Carol observed. "I wonder if Sheldon planned it that way, perhaps because he was trying to reconnect with Tara."

"I guess we'll just have to keep snooping and find out," Molly said.

Following her GPS, Molly steered onto a short dirt lane that led into thick woods that lined the loch. Most of the cabins on the road were empty at this time of year, although Molly saw smoke drifting from a couple of chimneys.

Tara's house was at the very end, a small cabin hunkered under towering pines. It was a cute place, its bright red shutters contrasting with dark wood siding. Flower boxes along the porch railing were lined with evergreen boughs and holly berries, a cheerful touch. A blue compact sedan was parked in front of a small shed that served as a garage.

"She's home," Molly said, parking her Honda Fit behind the sedan, careful to avoid the snowbanks encroaching on the edges of the driveway. She turned off the engine and the three women climbed out, Laura clutching a box of tarts.

They walked in single file up the narrow path onto the front porch, and Molly rang the bell. The curtain covering the front window flicked aside briefly, followed by the sound of locks clicking. Then the door opened, revealing Tara, who stood blinking up at them. Her brown hair was scraped up in a messy bun, and she wore sweatpants and a baggy sweater that dwarfed her slender frame.

Her mouth dropped open slightly. "Oh, I know you. You're from Bread on Arrival."

"We are," Molly said. "And we wanted to welcome you to Loch Mallaig."

Laura lifted the bakery box in demonstration.

Tara's gaze flitted from face to face. Finally, she stepped back. "Come in." She ran a hand over her hair. "Please excuse the mess. What do they say about the cobbler's kids? Well, you'd never know I was a housekeeper."

The cabin had one big room in front, with a short hallway leading to a few closed doors to the right and, at the back, an open doorway offering a glimpse of a kitchen beyond. Although furnished comfortably with a sofa and armchairs, the big room was indeed messy. Magazines and books were scattered over a large, square coffee table along with used mugs and glasses. Afghans were piled in a rumpled heap on the sofa, making Molly wonder if Tara had been napping. Outdoor equipment, including skis and snowshoes, was heaped in one corner.

"I know how it is," Carol said with her warm, reassuring laugh. "Working and raising a family is hard."

Tara threw Carol a glance of appreciation. "He's grown up now, but it's always been the two of us. Noah's dad wasn't ever in the picture." She gestured toward the furniture. "Have a seat. Does anyone want tea or coffee?"

They all requested tea, then Carol and Molly settled themselves on the sofa while Tara went to the kitchen, followed by Laura with the bakery box. Molly pushed the blankets aside. She considered folding them, but thought better of it, not wanting to appear critical. It was unfortunate they had obviously interrupted the woman's relaxation time.

A few minutes later, Tara and Laura emerged, Tara holding a tray of mugs and Laura a plate with tarts. Molly's mouth watered at the sight of the tarts, but she resolved not to eat another. Tara and her son should enjoy the privilege. After all, she would have first dibs when Laura baked them again.

With the gentle tinkle of spoons against ceramic, the women dunked tea bags and stirred in milk and sugar. Then, almost as one, they sat back with sighs.

"How do you like Loch Mallaig so far?" Carol asked.

Tara took a sip of tea. "I like it fine." She laughed. "It's quite a change from the city. Last night I heard an owl hooting—do you believe it?"

"I do," Laura said. "I live not too far from here. They hoot outside my house all the time."

"It's nice that you found a house close to the resort, Tara." Molly warmed her hands on her mug. "How's your job going?"

"Working at the resort is okay," Tara said, setting her mug on a coaster. "It's a great place, with nice people, and it was good of them to hire me when I haven't worked anywhere like it before. I'm an administrative assistant, but there isn't much market for that around here."

Molly's pulse leaped at Tara's mention of her career. "Tell us about your experience," she prompted. "We hear about job news all the time at the bakehouse. We can always keep an ear out."

"I worked in a handful of places," Tara said. "My longest job was at a veterinarian's office, which I really loved, but the doctor retired. Then I worked at a car dealership, a bank, and last, Barrie-Firth College." Her eyes flashed a challenge when she mentioned this last, and Molly could see a resemblance to her son's intense stare.

The three were silent a moment and then Carol said, "I think I heard something about the college." She waved a hand. "You know how small towns are."

Tara pressed her lips together, her cheeks flushing. "Yeah, I bet you did. That rat Finlay Croft fired me. I was ready to quit, but I hadn't found a new job yet. The man was impossible."

Tension fell over the room and Molly wondered how she could defuse it. If Tara guessed they were really here to fish for information, she would probably clam up.

"We could see that, Tara," Molly said, keeping her voice gentle. "And we barely knew the man."

"He really hurt my son too." Tara's voice was gravelly with unshed tears. "Noah felt like he had to drop out. And he was doing so well."

"I'm truly sorry to hear that," Laura said. "Our college student helper, Bridget, mentioned that Noah might be attending her school."

Tara's face lightened. "That's right. He went over there the other day to see what they offer and inquire about financial aid. He's planning to transfer credits." She cracked a small smile. "Maybe everything's going to be okay here now that—" She bit off the last word.

Now that Finlay was gone? Or was she relieved about Sheldon's demise?

The petite woman began to smooth her pants leg. "I don't talk about this much, and I'd appreciate it if what I tell you stays here." She glanced up, fixing them with those challenging eyes.

Molly's stomach felt cold. What secret was Tara about to divulge to them? Was she hiding something that protected a murderer?

15

Once everyone agreed to be discreet, Tara continued, "Sheldon and I used to date, back before Noah was born."

"That's why—" Laura blurted, before halting herself. "I mean, was he bothering you?" Her cheeks flamed with embarrassment at the slip. She'd almost revealed that they'd seen Tara and Sheldon in the college newspaper.

Tara studied Laura for a few seconds then said, "You could say that. Back in Marquette, after I bumped into him one day, the man wouldn't leave me alone. He befriended me on social media—which I never should have accepted—and he kept sending me messages. When I learned he'd moved here, I couldn't believe it. I thought I'd left him behind as well as my bad experience at the college."

The disgust Molly felt must have shown on her face, because Tara hastily added, "Oh, he never did or said anything out of line. He wanted to talk. He said that he regretted breaking up with me way back when. That he wasn't happy with . . ." She set her lips in a firm line. "You know what, I'm not going to go there. Sheldon is dead, and it won't help anything to talk about his marriage."

Tara didn't need to say more—Molly could read between the lines. Sheldon and Sheila had not been a happy pair.

"Did Sheila have any enemies?" Carol asked. "She seemed convinced that she was the target of the poison Sheldon drank."

"Not that I know of." Tara barked a short laugh. "Now, if I'd swallowed the poison, you could certainly suspect her. She really resented me. And you know what? I totally understand. It can be easier to blame someone else rather than examine what you're doing wrong. Their bad marriage was not my fault. I hadn't seen Sheldon for over twenty years when we bumped into each other."

Perhaps the very day captured by the roving college photographer, Molly thought. She turned to Carol. "Didn't you bring some Loch Mallaig brochures? Maybe Tara would like to take a peek, plan some activities with Noah."

This diversion eased the tension in the room, and the rest of the visit passed pleasantly enough. Soon they were driving away from the cabin.

"I hate to say this," Molly said. "But I keep wondering about Noah."

Laura leaned forward from the back seat. "Me too. He had the ability and the reason—two reasons, really—to be angry with Finlay."

Carol shook her head. "I hate to think it was really him. He's so young, his whole life ahead of him."

"True," Molly said. "But at that age, everything is felt so deeply. Setbacks can seem like the end of the world. And feeling forced to drop out of college is a big setback, especially with the emphasis placed on higher education these days."

"I agree," Laura said. "Here he is, waiting on tables and working at a bait shop instead of doing whatever he had planned. It must feel like a dead end."

The route back to the bakehouse led them past the fishing derby location. When Molly saw the banner advertising the contest, she asked, "Want to pop in and see how things are going?"

"Why don't we?" Carol agreed, and Molly knew she was eager to see Harvey.

Molly pulled into a spot in the parking lot. After pausing to put on hats and gloves, they got out of the car and walked toward the loch. Although the sun was out, a stinging wind blew into their faces, carrying powdery snow with it. The loch was also windswept, with areas blown clean to reveal blue ice.

Fergus stood on the shore talking to Vernon. He waved when he saw them. "Good afternoon. What brings you out here?"

Molly noticed Vernon was walking onto the ice and out of earshot, so she said, "We have some new information."

Fergus glanced over his shoulder at the loch, then at the cottage. "Why don't we go in and warm up? No one is inside right now."

The women followed the resort owner onto the porch, where they stamped their boots to dislodge snow from the treads, then into the toasty building. Fergus went to the woodstove and opened the door, then threw in another log. "It's a frosty one today," he said. "But the fishermen are all here. We haven't had a single dropout yet."

"Is Noah here?" Molly asked. She hadn't seen the young man on the grounds.

Fergus nodded. "He's doing the rounds on a snowmobile." His eyes sharpened. "Does your new information have to do with him?" He indicated they should sit on the benches. After unzipping his coat, he remained standing near the stove.

Molly sighed. "Yes it does. You remember what I told you before?" At his nod, she went on. "When we visited his mother this afternoon, we learned more about the connection between the Taggarts and Sheldon."

Fergus's brows rose. "What is it?"

"Tara and Sheldon used to date. Ages ago, before he got married." Molly paused. "Recently he was trying to rekindle a friendship after finding her on social media. He also claimed he was unhappily married."

Fergus rubbed his chin, considering this. "What did Tara think about that?"

"She wasn't interested," Carol said. "But apparently he was quite persistent, especially since they all lived here now."

"You think Noah might have gone after Sheldon?" Fergus surmised. "Because he was bothering his mother?"

It sounded like a thin reason, but murder wasn't rational. Sometimes emotions got out of hand, with situations feeling much larger and more devastating than they actually were. "Maybe there's more to it," Molly said. "We barely know Tara, so it could be that she held some details back."

"I can understand that," Laura said. "She doesn't know if we're going to gossip about her. And that's all she needs, as a newcomer to town."

Molly grimaced slightly. Technically they were discussing Tara's secret with someone after she specifically asked them not to—but catching a murderer seemed to take precedence over complete discretion at this point.

Fergus paced back and forth, thinking. Then the buzz of a snowmobile cut through the quiet. "Here comes Noah now. Maybe we should go have a word."

"All of us?" Carol asked. "Why don't you and Molly go? Laura and I will stay here and keep warm." She laughed. "I'm working myself up for the walk to Harvey's bob-house."

As Noah brought the machine to a stop near the weighing station, Fergus and Molly stepped out of the cottage.

"Hey, Noah," Fergus called. "How's it going out there?"

Noah climbed off his machine. "Fine. Fish are biting. They'll be coming in soon to weigh up."

When Fergus glanced at Molly, she realized he was waiting for her to broach the subject. "Noah, my friends and I went to see your mother today."

"Oh, yeah?" The young man's tone was instantly wary. "What for?"

"We wanted to welcome her to town," Molly said. "And we brought you both some plum tarts, a new recipe being featured at our bakehouse."

Noah continued to eye them, suspicion evident in his expression. His words were careful. "That was nice of you. Mom doesn't have many friends here yet."

Molly lowered her voice. "She told us about what happened in Marquette."

The young man's expression twisted with anger. "You mean how we were driven out of town by Finlay Croft? It wasn't bad enough that he fired Mom. He had the nerve to accuse me of cheating. Which I didn't do." He patted his chest. "Shot us both in the heart. He deserved to die the same way." Horror flashed over his face as he realized what he had just said. Before they could stop him, he jumped onto the snowmobile, started the engine, and took off.

Molly stood, stunned, watching the machine race across the snow-covered lake. "Do you think that was a confession?"

"I don't know, but it certainly could be interpreted as one," Fergus said grimly. "We'd better call the police."

"Where do you think he's going?" Molly asked as Noah receded into the distance. He was already halfway across the cove.

Fergus had his phone out and was tapping at the screen. "There's a whole network of trails you can tap into on the other side. He could be going anywhere from here to Canada."

While Fergus placed his call, Molly kept her eyes fastened on the snowmobile, wanting to see where Noah left the loch. That could tell the police where he might be found.

"They're on the alert," Fergus said as he hung up. "I'm supposed to call back with more information, like where he goes."

"I'm watching him." Molly pointed. "See? He's close to the shore over there."

Fergus gave a shout of alarm. "There's a channel right where he's heading. The ice there is thin. If Noah falls in . . ."

He didn't need to say more. Molly already knew that icy water could cause deadly hypothermia in minutes. If Noah didn't drown first, the plunge of his core temperature would kill him.

As if Fergus's words were prophetic, Noah's snowmobile slowed with a sputter. Without warning, the machine began to sink, deep black water opening around the vehicle as the ice broke.

"He's gone through the ice!" she shouted. "Fergus, he's going to die!"

16

Fergus bounded to the weigh station, where he rang a hanging bell. *Clang, clang, clang.* As fishermen burst out of the bob-houses, he grabbed a bullhorn from a lower shelf. "SOS. Man through the ice. SOS."

Molly watched in awe as the men hurried to help, including Fergus, who ran down to the ice, and Vernon, who directed the others. A couple of fishermen jumped on snowmobiles while others found rope and tossed it to those on the machines. Another hooked a gurney sled to the back of a machine and strapped a first aid kit on top. But would they be in time? She could see Noah's head bobbing in the dark water.

Carol and Laura ran outside to join Molly. "What's going on?" Carol asked. "We heard the bell ringing. What was Fergus saying through the bullhorn?"

"Noah took off on his snowmobile and went through the ice." Molly clenched her fists and tears stung her eyes. "And it's all my fault. Fergus and I were questioning him and he got upset."

"It is not your fault," Laura said stoutly. "He chose to drive across the lake, right? He went the wrong way by accident."

"People fall through the ice all the time," Carol said. "Harvey's told me about it. Noah didn't know the loch well enough."

Despite their well-meaning reassurances, Molly's heart ached with fear and regret. Maybe Noah hadn't known the safe spots on the loch, but it was her fault he had fled in the first place. She clenched her jaw and prayed as the fleet of snowmobiles zoomed toward the dangerous spot. Not only was Noah in jeopardy, but trying to rescue him would put the other fishermen at risk. They might fall through the ice too.

Laura put a pair of binoculars up to her eyes and focused on the distant scene.

"Where did you get those?" Molly asked.

"I found them inside." Laura handed the binoculars to Molly. "Here. The snowmobile must have had a flotation device."

Carol nodded. "Harvey says all the snowmobiles have them just for situations like this."

Molly scanned the lake until she found the spot. Noah was clinging to a floating tube, keeping as much of his torso out of the water as possible. Racing across the lake, raising a wake of powdery snow behind them, the other snowmobiles were drawing closer. In only a minute or two, they would reach him.

Fergus hurried up the bank toward them. "We've got an ambulance coming. They're going to bring him back here." He nodded thanks when Molly gave him the binoculars. "There's no road access over there. It's all swamp and woods."

The group watched in tense silence while the fishermen carried out the rescue operation. They threw a rope to Noah, who clung to it for dear life. Once they pulled him out of the water onto stable ice, they bundled him up and put him on the gurney, smothered in blankets. Then the convoy of snowmobiles raced back over the white expanse to the near shore.

Flashing lights along the road announced the arrival of the ambulance and a police cruiser. Chief Thomson picked his way down to the waterfront, followed by Officer Greer Anderson and a pair of EMTs lugging their own gurney.

"Perfect timing," Fergus called. "They're on their way back."

Chief Thomson stared out at the lake, giving a satisfied nod when he saw the approaching snowmobiles. "They get him out pretty fast?"

"Yes," Molly said. "He was probably only in the water about five minutes."

The paramedics exchanged glances. "Good news," one said. "Considering the current lake temperature, he would have been unconscious in a few more minutes."

And if he'd passed out, Molly reflected, it would have been extremely difficult to get him out of the water without jeopardizing the rescuers.

The snowmobiles roared closer. The medical personnel carried the gurney down to the lake, prepared to load up their patient and whisk him away. Chief Thomson, Officer Anderson, and Fergus followed behind.

"Let's go down." Laura motioned for Molly to follow along. "I want to find out how he is."

Molly did as well, but her guilt at causing Noah's flight still lingered. She was beyond grateful that he was alive and hopefully on his way to a full recovery.

Carol put a gloved hand on Molly's jacket sleeve. "It's okay, Molly. No one is blaming you. I doubt Noah would even think to."

Noah has other things to worry about, like being arrested for murder. That thought didn't make Molly feel any better, but she ended up going with Laura and Carol down to the loch.

Harvey came to greet them. "We got there just in time. He was fading fast."

Carol gave her husband a hug. "My hero. I'm so proud of you." Harvey's smile was self-deprecating, but Molly could tell he was pleased by her praise.

The snowmobiles had arrived, and the EMTs were already bent over Noah, talking to him and assessing his condition. As the Bakehouse

Three reached the scene, the paramedics picked Noah up and transferred him to the ambulance gurney.

Sam, the visiting fisherman Laura had danced with, gathered up Noah's clothing and stuffed it into a nylon gear sack. "This stuff is freezing stiff already," he commented. He noticed Laura and nodded a greeting. She gave him a small wave.

"You all did a great job," one paramedic said. "Getting him out of wet clothes and into a thick, dry sleeping bag right away probably saved his life." The paramedics began wheeling the gurney across the packed snow. A couple of fishermen went along in case they needed help when they reached the snow-covered path.

"What happened?" Chief Thomson asked the group. "Anyone see?"

"I was in my bob-house with Vernon," Harvey said. "We heard a snowmobile, and when we glanced out, we saw it tearing across the lake. Didn't think anything of it until Fergus rang the bell."

Everyone's focus shifted to Fergus. "Molly and I were talking to Noah," he said. "He got upset and took off." He gave the chief a significant look, and Molly hoped the chief would understand there was more to the story. "We were watching because he headed right for where the ice is weak. After we saw him break through, I roused the troops with the bell and they went after him."

"Many fishermen are trained in lake rescue techniques," Vernon said. "Safety is *verra* important, summer or winter."

"Noah was fortunate then," Greer said. "If no one had seen him fall into the lake or if help was delayed . . ." She didn't need to finish the sentence. They all knew the grim outcome the young man had so narrowly avoided.

A thought hit Molly. "We need to tell his mother." She would want to be informed immediately if something happened to Chloe.

Fergus appeared stricken. "You're right." He glanced at the time on his phone. "Tara must be at work by now." He stepped aside a short distance to call the resort. While he was talking, Chief Thomson interviewed the fishermen who had gone to Noah's rescue, including the men who helped escort him to the ambulance. Then they returned to their bob-houses to continue fishing.

Fergus rejoined the group, tucking his phone in his jacket pocket. "Neil is going to drive Tara to the hospital." He shook his head and rubbed his face with one hand. "That was one of the hardest calls I've ever made."

"But at least it was relatively good news," Molly said. "After all, he's going to be okay."

"They think so anyway." Greer glanced at her boss. "Think I should head over to the hospital, keep an eye on things?"

"I do," the chief said. "I'll meet you there in a while." He tilted his head at Molly and Fergus. "I want to hear exactly what happened."

"That's our cue," Carol said, touching Harvey's arm. "Why don't we show Laura your bob-house?"

Vernon headed into the cabin while Laura and the MacCallans started across the lake toward Harvey's bob-house. Once he was alone with Fergus and Molly, Chief Thomson said, "Tell me what made him run."

Molly and Fergus traded off taking the chief through the sequence of events. "I feel so guilty," Molly said once the story was relayed. "Mentioning Marquette really upset him."

Chief Thomson's keen gaze examined Molly. "You couldn't have predicted such an extreme reaction, Molly. And if he hadn't chosen that route, he would have safely made it to the other shore. He might be miles away by now."

"That's true," Fergus added. "There's a big system that ties in right over there."

Their words relieved Molly's burden of guilt, but only slightly. She swallowed. "Do you think he might have killed Finlay?"

The chief folded his arms over his chest. "All I'll say is that once Noah is alert enough, we will question him. I hope that's satisfactory to you."

Molly's cheeks would have burned if they weren't already frozen. "Of course, Chief. I wasn't trying to interfere." Her motive had been to uncover helpful information, which she had. The more they learned, the sooner they would all discover the truth.

Chief Thomson adjusted his hat. "I'd better be on my way. Good day to you both." He gave them a brief smile then began to trudge through the snow toward the parking lot.

"Don't waste time on regret, Molly," Fergus said. "You and I know that Brodie was framed. If we let it go, then a killer will win."

Molly squared her shoulders. "I appreciate you saying that, Fergus. Now I'd better go get Carol and Laura. We need to get back to the bakery. Hamish is closing, but we still have a few things to do."

As Molly stepped onto the snow-covered ice, Carol and Laura emerged from Harvey's bob-house. She stopped to wait for them.

"Hey Molly," Carol said as she drew closer. "Want to come over for dinner tonight? I'm making shepherd's pie."

"And I'm bringing homemade rolls," Laura said. "I found a new recipe I want to try."

Molly hadn't thought about dinner yet, so the invitation was welcome. "I'd love that." After mentally reviewing the contents of her refrigerator, she said, "I can bring a green salad."

"Perfect," Carol said. She fell into step with Molly and Laura as they walked up the slight slope to the parking lot. "How's six o'clock? That will give Harvey time to get home and cleaned up."

They climbed into Molly's car and set off, soon arriving downtown.

As they drove down Tattie Bogle Road, Molly saw Brodie shoveling snow in front of Neeps and Tatties. Although they hadn't gotten new snowfall, a good amount had drifted over the restaurant walkway.

"Who wants to give Brodie an update?" Molly asked once she was parked in the bakery lot.

"I do," Laura offered, opening her door. "He'll be interested, I'm sure."

As the three women crossed the street, Brodie stopped shoveling and waved. Then he waited with gloved hands resting on the handle for them to reach him. He wore a hat pulled low, his cheeks, nose, and chin red with cold. "Good afternoon," he said. "How are you ladies doing today?"

"We're fine," Molly said. "We wanted to give you a quick update." She paused, formulating her words. "Did you hear that Noah Taggart fell through the ice today?"

To her surprise, he nodded. "Noah's mother called us and said he wouldn't make it to work tonight. She told me he's going to be in the hospital overnight, but other than that, he'll be okay."

Carol and Laura expressed relief, and Molly released a breath she hadn't realized she was holding. "I'm glad to hear that," Molly said. "We were there when it happened."

Brodie's brows rose in surprise. "Really? I understand it happened out at the fishing derby."

"That's right," Molly said glumly. "After Fergus and I talked to him and Finlay Croft came up. Both Noah and his mother had major problems with Finlay. And Noah was on the archery team at Barrie-Firth."

The ex-fireman was an intelligent man, and he caught on immediately. "So you think *Noah* might have killed Finlay." He shook his head. "Wow, I didn't see that coming. He's a good kid." He paused. "I thought."

"I know." Molly's chest tightened with misery. "The police are going to question him about Finlay, so we'll see what happens." After a pause, she mused out loud, "But I don't see a connection to Sheldon. I mean, Tara knew him ages ago, but why would Noah be upset about that?" She bit the words off. The only possible conclusion was that Noah wanted to get Sheldon out of his mother's life—permanently.

"Oh, Noah wouldn't hurt Sheldon," Brodie said. He scooped up a pile of snow and tossed it. "He said Sheldon was his father."

17

"Would you like seconds?" Carol asked Molly. "I'm asking before Harvey eats all the shepherd's pie."

"It's one of my favorite winter meals," Harvey said, scraping up the last bite from his plate.

Molly dragged her attention back to the dinner table, realizing she'd drifted off again. Ever since they'd spoken to Brodie this afternoon, she'd mulled over his words in her mind. *Noah believes Sheldon is his father.*

Maybe it *was* true. "So who killed Sheldon, then?"

Realizing she'd spoken aloud—and hadn't answered Carol's question—Molly clapped a hand over her mouth. "Sorry, I guess I'm a little preoccupied." But that hadn't prevented her from eating everything, she noticed. She picked up the empty plate and handed it to Carol. "Yes, I would love more shepherd's pie. But only a spoonful. I'd be a poor guest if I didn't save some for Harvey."

As Carol scooped Molly's seconds from the serving dish, Laura buttered a roll. "Still thinking about what Brodie said?" She sighed. "I can't get it out of my mind."

"Neither can I," Carol said. "If Sheldon was his father, then Noah has suffered a real tragedy." She made a clucking sound. "Losing his dad like that."

"Yeah, that's quite a loss for someone so young," Harvey agreed. "Are you going to find out if it's true?"

"I suppose we could pay another visit to Tara and ask," Carol said as she handed Molly the replenished plate.

"What will our excuse be this time?" Molly asked, scooping up a bite of ground beef, creamed corn, and fluffy mashed potatoes. This dish was so delicious, she ought to make it for herself more often.

Under the table, Angus bumped against her legs as if he could read her mind about the tasty dinner she was enjoying. She resolved to save him a bite. He liked coming here, although he'd never been able to make friends with Carol's gray-and-white striped cat, Pascal. The shy kitty was presently hanging out under Carol's bed, as usual.

"I think we'll tell her the truth," Carol said. "That we're looking into Sheldon's death. Even if Noah did kill Finlay, I doubt he poisoned his supposed father. I know that sort of thing happens sometimes, but based on what Brodie said, it seems unlikely in this case."

"When do you think you'll go?" Laura pulled out her phone to check her calendar. "I have a doctor's appointment tomorrow and after that, I'll be really busy at the bakehouse."

"Tara probably goes to work at three," Molly said as she and Carol glanced at each other. "Say early afternoon? Bridget comes in at eleven, so she can cover for us."

"You two go over," Laura said. "Two visitors are way less intimidating than three. Maybe you'll learn more this time."

Molly relaxed with a sigh, glad to have formulated a plan of action. Tonight was for spending time with her friends, she reminded herself. They often got together like this for a casual evening meal, but after decades living apart, it was still precious every time they could enjoy a fun night in.

"Who's up for a game of Scrabble after dinner?" Harvey asked, his eyes twinkling. He rubbed his hands together with glee at the prospect.

"That sounds fun," Laura said. "I haven't played in ages."

"I'm warning you, Harvey is brilliant at Scrabble," Carol said. "I think he's memorized the dictionary."

"I'm not too shabby myself," Molly said. "So you'd better bring your A game, Harvey." They all laughed, a beautiful sound.

Before the midday rush started the next morning, Molly called Tara. "How is Noah?" Molly asked when the other woman answered. "I was at the loch when he had his accident."

"You were?" Tara said, sounding eager. "What happened? No one has really given me any details." Her tone grew bitter. "Not even the police. They wouldn't let me in the room when they talked to him."

That must have been awful. "Are you going to be around this afternoon? I don't have time to chat now, but I can stop by later." She could fill Tara in about the incident, then bring up Sheldon again, and, if all went well, mention Noah's theory about his paternity. Remembering Tara had once worked for a veterinarian and might like animals, she added, "If you want, I can bring my dog over. He's an expert at cheering people up."

She heard the smile in Tara's voice. "That sounds great. How about around one? I'm going to the hospital at two to pick him up. Fortunately I'm off today."

"I'm so glad he's being released," Molly said honestly. "One o'clock it is. See you then."

After the noon rush subsided, Carol and Molly left the bakehouse in Laura and Bridget's capable hands and drove out to Tara's house with Angus. Molly had a knot in her stomach. She hated to discuss possibly intrusive subjects with people she barely knew, but how else were they going to get to the bottom of the situation? If they sat back and did nothing, it was likely that a good man would go to jail for life. Not that Molly blamed the police or the prosecutor.

They had to follow the evidence trail, and so far it unfortunately led to Brodie.

As their route to Tara's house went past Sheldon and Sheila's house, Molly peeked down the driveway and saw a sleek, white SUV with its back hatch open and several boxes inside. "Looks like Sheila is doing some early spring cleaning."

"Probably boxing up Sheldon's belongings," Carol said. "I wonder how she's doing, really. We should visit her today too. She must be reeling from losing her husband."

Molly, who spoke from experience, said, "I'm sure she is. It takes a while to feel normal again."

In a reprise of the day before, Molly pulled into Tara's driveway and parked behind her sedan. Carol grabbed a box of treats for Noah's homecoming, and Molly clipped a leash on Angus and let him sniff his way toward the front door.

"Oh, what a cute dog!" Tara said when she opened the door. "Come on in."

After stepping through the door, Molly unclipped the leash, allowing Angus to scamper to Tara to make friends.

"You are so sweet!" Tara exclaimed, crouching to scratch his ears. "I didn't realize how much I missed being around animals since I stopped working for the vet."

Carol held up the box. "These are for Noah and you."

"How kind," Tara said. She straightened and accepted the box from Carol. "Really, you don't have to bring treats every time you visit."

"In this case, we thought it would be a nice get-well gesture." Carol unzipped her coat. "Nothing speeds healing like yummy baked goods."

Tara carried the box toward the kitchen. "That's certainly true. Have a seat and I'll put on some tea."

Molly and Carol settled on the sofa, and Molly patted her thighs.

"Angus, come." He ran over and curled up next to her ankles. "Good boy." Molly patted his head.

Tara soon emerged, carrying a tray with mugs and a selection of tea bags plus milk and sugar. She set her burden on the coffee table, then took a seat in a nearby chair. "Help yourself."

This time, Molly chose a chamomile blend. She'd had enough caffeine today already, and her nerves were plenty active as it was. She placed the tea bag in the hot water and left it to steep. "I'm so relieved that Noah is all right," she said, a soft way to broach the subject.

With her mug cradled in her hands, Tara faced Molly, her expression eager. "Tell me what happened. Why on earth was he driving across thin ice?"

"The answer to that is easy," Molly said. "He wasn't familiar with the loch, so he didn't know the ice was thin. Fergus told me that a channel runs under the ice in that spot, but it was hidden by a blanket of thick snow. Anyone could make that mistake."

"Fortunately fishermen trained in water rescue were on hand to help," Carol said. "They had him out of the water in, what, five minutes or so?"

"That's right," Molly said. "They were amazing."

"But what happened before that?" Tara's anguish poked at Molly's conscience. "Where was he going? And why?" She set her mug on the table, her full attention on Molly.

Molly swallowed. How much should she say? She glanced at Carol, who gave her a little nod. Honesty was the best policy, right? "I'm not sure of his destination," she said. "But he was upset after talking with me. I mentioned Finlay Croft's name."

Tara stiffened, her face a mask of shock, and Molly backtracked.

"Actually, that's not quite right. I mentioned Marquette. He's the one who brought up Finlay." As she had expected he would, she admitted to herself. The nerves she was trying to settle tightened in trepidation.

Tara's mouth twisted. "Of course he did. Noah blames Finlay for ruining our lives." The woman's scowl revealed that she blamed the deceased professor as well. A sudden awareness flashed in her eyes, and she shot to her feet. "Are they going to try and pin Finlay's murder on Noah?"

Molly leaned back in response to the woman's looming figure. Angus jumped up with a yelp and scrambled away. "The police don't pin things on people here. They examine the evidence."

Tara sank back into her chair. "I suppose that's true. Just because you don't like someone, that isn't enough for the police to arrest you, is it?"

Trying to change the subject—or at least hoping she wouldn't actually make the situation worse—Molly said, "Noah thinks Sheldon was his father." At his mother's stunned expression, she added, "Or so he told his boss."

Tara bit her bottom lip as she shook her head. "Oh no, Sheldon wasn't his father. We broke up before I met and married Noah's dad. But he died in a car accident before Noah was born."

"I'm sorry," Carol said, her voice full of sympathy. "That must have been so difficult."

"It was. Really, really hard." Tara gave a nod of acknowledgment. "I had no idea Noah was thinking that. But I suppose it makes sense. He never knew his father, and there was good old Sheldon, back in the picture. Or trying to be," she amended. She picked up her mug again. "I'll have to set him straight."

Now that things had calmed down, Angus came back to the sofa. When he settled next to her, Molly noticed he had something in his teeth. "Drop it," she said, gently tugging on the strap of a pair of goggles.

Then she realized something. They had green lenses, like the pairs she had seen while researching night-hunting equipment.

Molly glanced up to find Tara's gaze fixed on her. Something flashed between the women—a shared knowledge of the truth. A chill ran down Molly's spine.

The person who killed Finlay lived in this house.

18

Tara reached for the eyewear and tried to tug it out of Molly's grasp, eliciting a growl from Angus. The woman pulled harder, lips twisted in a grim sneer. Then she suddenly let go and bolted for the door, grabbing a coat and pulling car keys out of the pocket.

"Stop!" Carol cried. "Running away won't do you any good."

But Tara didn't respond to Carol's plea. Instead, she opened the door and, leaving it ajar, ran outside. A moment later, the roar of an engine starting filtered into the house.

"What should we do?" Carol rose to her feet. "She's getting away."

"She can't go far." Molly got up to close the door against the chilly air pouring inside, nudging a curious Angus out of the way with her foot. "We're blocking her in." She watched out the window as Tara drove forward a few feet, then turned her wheel to the right, attempting to take her car across the snowy lawn.

"I'm calling the police," Carol said, fumbling for her phone. "Maybe they can track her down." She hastily dialed 911.

The snowbanks lining the drive were deep, and Tara's car was soon hung up on a heap of snow, the wheels spinning helplessly. After revving the engine a few times, she abandoned the vehicle and ran to Molly's car.

With a lurch of panic, Molly checked her coat pocket. *Phew*. She had her car keys, and she remembered locking her doors on their way to the front door. Thinking fast, she locked the house front door, then ran through the kitchen to the back door and secured that too. The last thing they needed was a confrontation with a killer—or someone trying to protect one.

Tara's actions left no doubt in Molly's mind that she or Noah had killed Finlay. Now she was hoping to escape, either on her own or after picking up her son from the hospital.

Molly peered out the front window again. Tara was sprinting down the driveway, arms and legs pumping. There really wasn't any place for her to go out here. It was a low-traffic area with few residents. Then again, there were plenty of people congregated at the fishing derby. One of the fishermen might take pity on her and give her a ride. That wouldn't be good.

Molly dug in her handbag for her phone. Angus watched her every move, whining in anxiety. "I know, boy. This is a bad situation."

"Where is Tara now?" Carol called, still on the phone with the dispatcher.

"She's running down the road toward the resort."

Molly's fingers curled around her phone. She pulled it out and dialed Fergus. He was judging again and hopefully would hear the call. If not, she would try Harvey or Vernon.

Her knees wobbled when Fergus actually picked up. "Oh, Fergus. I'm so glad you answered."

"I always do when you call, don't I?" Laughter colored his voice. "If I can."

"Fergus, I'm calling to warn you," she said, infusing seriousness into her voice. "Tara Taggart is headed your way, and I think she's dangerous."

A surprised silence met her words. "What do you mean by dangerous? What is she driving?"

"She's on foot." Molly gave him a quick rundown. "We called the police but it will take them time to get out here. I thought she might approach someone at the tournament and ask for a ride, tell them her car broke down or something."

"Yes, that would be a good ploy," Fergus agreed. "Thanks for calling. I'd better go. Stay in touch, okay? And be safe."

Molly returned to the couch, Angus at her heels.

"The police are on their way," Carol said.

"Good." Molly sat down beside her friend, using the edge of an afghan to pick up the night vision goggles and move them to the coffee table. "And I called Fergus to warn him that she might be headed their way."

"What do we do now?" Carol asked, picking up her mug with shaking hands.

"Nothing," Molly said. "Sit here and wait. The police will want to see those goggles."

Carol set down the mug with a clink. "I wonder if Noah or Tara killed Sheldon. They were both at the community center that night."

"It's certainly a possibility," Molly said miserably. "Although I didn't sense any great animosity when Tara was talking about Sheldon. More annoyance than anything."

"Maybe she was hiding her true feelings," Carol said. "After all, this is the woman who stood back and let Brodie take the blame for Finlay."

"You're right." Molly's core tightened with anger and revulsion. She wanted nothing more than to get out of Tara's house. Her feet itching to move, she jumped up. In response, Angus got to his feet and stared up at her.

"What are you doing?" Carol asked.

"I don't know. I feel like pacing to try and burn off some of my angst." Then Molly realized she shouldn't move around the room. "But I'd better not. Anything we do in here might mess up some evidence." It was bad enough that the goggles had Angus's teeth marks on the strap. She sank back onto the sofa. "I sure hope the police get here fast."

With frequent checking of her phone, Molly determined that fifteen minutes had gone by before a cruiser pulled into the yard. Molly went to the front door and unlocked it, watching while Officers Greer Anderson and Dalziel Murdoch got out of the cruiser. They retrieved crime scene kits from the trunk, then started for the cabin.

"Everything all right in there?" Officer Anderson called.

"We're fine," Molly answered. "It's just me and Carol. Did you locate Tara Taggart yet?"

Greer shook her head. "Not yet. We're calling in other departments to help search."

"I hope they find her soon," Molly said, not only talking about Tara's probable guilt. In this weather, time was of the essence. Staying outside in frigid temperatures could kill almost as quickly as being immersed in cold water.

"She's now our primary suspect in the murder of Finlay Croft," Officer Murdoch said. "Why else would she have run when you found the night vision goggles?"

Molly concurred with that theory. She backed into the cabin so the officers could enter. "We didn't touch anything. Well, except the goggles that Angus discovered. They're on the coffee table." As if in answer, Angus yipped. He ran to greet the officers. Molly scooped him up. "Sorry. I'll keep him out of your way."

Carol had risen to her feet. "I'm so glad you're here. The whole thing was quite a surprise—Angus finding the goggles and Tara running off."

"Why don't you tell us about that?" Officer Anderson prompted.

Molly sat down with Angus in the closest chair. "Carol and I were at the loch when Noah Taggart fell through the ice. We were here to

deliver some baked goods. He was supposed to come home today."
Noah. Molly's heart twisted with pity for the young man.

"Oh, the poor thing!" Carol cried. "He's waiting at the hospital
for his mother."

The officers exchanged glances. "We'll make sure Noah is taken care
of," Greer said. "Excuse me a moment." She stepped into the kitchen
and placed a call. When she returned, she told Murdoch, "We're
stationing a guard at the hospital." She perched on an ottoman near
Molly. "Let's keep going. So you were here visiting." Her voice held a
note of justified skepticism.

"We were concerned about Noah," Molly said. "He was telling
people that Sheldon Barker was his father. His mother wasn't aware
that he thought so. And, according to her, Sheldon wasn't Noah's
father. She had been married, but her husband died."

Greer accepted the explanation without further comment. "Tell
me about the goggles."

"We were visiting Laura Donovan's parents the other day," Molly
explained, "and her father made a good point. He said it would be hard
for someone to shoot a target at night without night vision gear." She
quickly added, "We were watching a story about Finlay on the news
at the time."

Again the officers looked at each other. When they remained
silent, Molly continued, "As you know, Officer Anderson, I was there
when the bow and arrows were discovered at Brodie's house. But I
didn't see any night vision equipment. Today, we were sitting here
drinking tea when Angus found those goggles, I'm guessing in that
pile of outdoor equipment over there. He dragged them over and
gave them to me."

"Smart dog," Officer Murdoch murmured.

"He is," Molly said. "He also can be quite mischievous." She ruffled his fur. "Can't you, Angus?" In this case, she was thankful that he'd nosed around where he shouldn't.

"What happened after he found the goggles?" Greer asked.

Molly took a breath and thought back. "I think Tara recognized the night vision goggles at the same time I did." Her cheeks heated. "I mean, I thought that's what they must be since the lenses are green. She tried to snatch them away from Angus, which he tends to see as a game. Then she gave up and ran out of the house."

"We were blocking her in." Carol took up the tale. "So she tried to get around us but got stuck. Then she took off on foot. I called the police and Molly called Fergus."

Officer Anderson lifted a brow. "And why would you call Fergus?"

"I thought Tara might go toward where they're hosting the fishing tournament," Molly said. "Since she didn't have a vehicle, she might ask someone for a ride. And who wouldn't help a woman who's alone on foot in the winter?"

"Very good point," Officer Murdoch said. "Quick thinking."

"Any other details?" Officer Anderson said. When Molly and Carol shook their heads, she glanced at her phone with a grunt of satisfaction. "The warrant is approved. We're going to search the premises. You two head home."

"Would one of you mind moving your cruiser so we can get out?" Molly asked.

"Sure," Murdoch said, jingling the keys.

Carol and Molly gathered their things and put on their coats and boots, leashed Angus, then followed the officer outside. The sun was already starting to sink on the short January day, and their breath was clearly visible in the frosty air. Angus pranced along, not liking the feel of the icy path on his paws.

"I sure hope you find Tara soon," Molly said to Officer Murdoch.

"Me too," he replied. "This isn't the kind of day you want to be outside for long unless you're dressed for it." He hopped into the cruiser and backed out of the driveway, where he waited until Molly had backed out. Then he pulled back in.

Molly was about to drive down the road when she saw Officer Murdoch wave. She halted, waiting until he trotted over to them. She rolled down the window a crack.

The young officer bent over, his brown eyes earnest. "You two be careful, okay? Until Tara Taggart is arrested, all citizens need to be on the lookout."

"We will," Molly promised, swallowing a stab of fear. Would Tara come after them, blaming them for setting the police on her? It wouldn't be rational, but what killer was? She checked to be sure all the doors were locked.

"And if you see any sign of her, anything at all, you call us," the officer went on. "Don't try to be heroes."

Carol leaned forward so he could see her face. "That's the last thing we want to do, Officer Murdoch. Thanks for your help."

He gave them a brisk nod and wished them good day, then turned and strode back toward the cabin. Molly stepped on the gas.

"Wow," Carol said, leaning back against the seat. "What a day." She took out her phone. "I'm going to send Laura an update. I don't know if she'll be glad or mad that she missed the excitement."

"You never know," Molly said. "As for me, I just as soon would have skipped it." Her gaze scanned both sides of the road as she drove. What if she spotted Tara hiding in the woods? Or what if she'd broken into one of the empty cabins? She tried to remember which ones had been occupied on the way up the lane.

She slowed in front of one house, where a thin thread of smoke was coming from the chimney. She didn't see any vehicles in the yard.

Then an elderly man emerged from the house, tugging on a cap. He trudged toward the mailbox. When he raised a bushy, white eyebrow at her, she waved and sped up.

Carol was still busy with her phone. "What are you doing?"

"I thought maybe . . . oh, never mind." But Molly continued to scan the surroundings. Tara had to be somewhere around here, unless she'd tried to hitchhike and been picked up already. Doing so was dangerous, but Tara was no doubt desperate.

They reached the end of the lane and Molly turned right to head back toward town. "Want to stop and see Harvey?" she asked. Maybe they could also get an update from Fergus if he knew more than they did.

"Sure," Carol said. "I'll send him a message that we're coming."

As she had on the way to Tara's, Molly glanced down the driveway to the Barker house. The SUV still sat in the same spot, but the rear hatch was closed now. An awful thought struck her. What if Tara had tried to confront Sheila? If Sheila was the intended victim and Tara had put the poison in the cup, then maybe . . .

Molly could call the police, of course, but they were already nearby. She found herself turning into the driveway, in a sudden maneuver that made the tires slip a little on the ice. Angus let out an anxious yip and Carol glanced up from her phone. "What are we doing?"

"I think we need to check on Sheila and make sure she's all right." Molly gripped the steering wheel so hard her fingers hurt. "She might be in danger."

19

Molly accelerated down the long driveway, eager to reach the house. She might be overreacting, but it wouldn't hurt to check on Sheila. They'd be in and out in less than a minute, she expected.

"You really think Tara might have come over here?" Carol asked.

"It's a possibility," Molly said, braking to a stop behind the white SUV. "It's not that far from her house and certainly closer than the fishing derby. That could be why no one has seen her."

Carol pursed her lips. "Should we call the police?"

"Not yet," Molly decided. "They're pretty busy. But if we see even one thing that seems wrong, we certainly will."

Carol reached for the door handle with a sigh. "I hope we find them sitting together drinking tea."

Molly laughed. "I'm afraid I doubt that. I'm sure Sheila won't be happy to learn that her husband had been talking to an ex-girlfriend. If she finds out about it, that is," she amended. She grabbed her cell phone from her purse and slid it into her coat pocket along with her keys. No way was she leaving them in her car, not while Tara was on the loose.

Angus whined in the back seat, clearly sensing that his mistress was about to get out of the car.

"We won't be long, boy," Molly told him. "You'll be fine right here." He settled down with a snort, head on his paws.

Carol and Molly walked along a short flagstone path to the front door, which was set in a shallow recess serving as an entrance. Molly peered through the sidelight and saw only a blurry hallway through the beveled glass. She rang the bell, which chimed a greeting audible even outside.

"Loud doorbell," Carol commented.

No one came in response to the summons, so Molly rang again, hoping Sheila wasn't napping or taking a shower. *Or being held hostage.*

This time someone shouted, "Hold on. I'm coming."

Molly peeked through the window again and saw a figure hurrying their way.

The front door cracked open and Sheila peered out. Surprise was followed by confusion, then, finally, a wan smile. Sheila sniffed. "How did you know?"

Molly sent Carol a puzzled look. "Know what?"

Tears began to roll down the widow's face. "I was sitting here, feeling so lonely and forlorn, without a friend in the world. And then you two angels show up."

Oh boy. Molly groaned inwardly. So much for the quick visit she'd planned.

"What can we do to help?" the ever-sympathetic Carol asked. "Want to talk?"

Molly inhaled. "What about Harvey?" she asked, speaking out of the side of her mouth.

"He'll be fine," Carol said. "As long as he's fishing, he's happy." She moved forward, obviously planning to accept Sheila's invitation.

"I'd better get Angus then," Molly said, glancing over her shoulder at the car. In these cold temperatures, she couldn't leave him in there. Any residual heat would soon evaporate.

"Come on in when you're ready," Sheila said. "We'll be in the kitchen."

The door shut behind Carol and Sheila, and Molly went back to the car. Somehow realizing what was happening, Angus began to leap about the back seat in excitement.

"Hold on, hold on," she told the wriggling dog as she tried to fasten his leash. "You be a good boy in there, okay?"

The Barker house was ringed by trees, and Molly's gaze was drawn to the dark woods. Was Tara out there, watching her? *Surely not. She'd be freezing by now.*

Pushing aside her fears, Molly walked Angus around the yard for a minute before leading him to the house. Inside the front door, she dried his paws on the mat, then removed her boots and put them next to Carol's.

Voices drifted from the kitchen, but she took a moment to glance around. The house was spacious, with large rooms to each side of the hallway. The veined marble tile underfoot appeared expensive and perfectly suited the home's tasteful color palette of grays, white, and blues.

Molly and Angus followed the voices to the kitchen, where Carol and Sheila sat on stools at a granite island. Everything in here was new and expensive too—the huge stainless steel refrigerator, the six-burner stove, the glass-front cabinets full of dishes. There was no sign that anyone else had been here. No coats, boots, or dirty coffee mugs.

"You have a beautiful home," Molly said, pulling out a stool at the island. Big multipaned windows offered a view of the deck and backyard, which was edged by the woods. A small building stood to one side, a path shoveled to its bright blue door.

"Thank you," Sheila said. "I decorated it myself." She swiveled on her stool and pointed to a one-cup maker on the counter near the stove. "Feel free to make coffee or tea."

"What are you drinking?" Molly asked Carol.

"Mocha." Carol lifted her mug. "It's really good."

Molly went over to the counter and studied the array of choices. "I think I'll try that too." She selected the right pod and popped it into the machine. "So, Sheila, how are you doing?"

The recent widow sighed heavily. "I really need to get away, you know? With all that's happened—well, I can't even *sleep* in this house. Too many memories."

"I can understand that," Carol said. "The reminders must be hard."

"They are." Sheila paused. "And the weather has been so awful. I need somewhere warm and sunny, like Florida."

The maker hissed and spit, then cocoa-infused coffee began to gurgle into Molly's mug. "We all do right about now," Molly said. "This has been a terrible winter."

"You got that right. There are so many lovely places to be this time of year." Sheila started naming some of the ones she'd visited, such as Orlando, Miami, and Key West.

Molly was still waiting for her hot drink to finish brewing, and her curious gaze fell on the refrigerator. Like most people, Sheila and Sheldon had pinned various items to it, including postcards, menus from restaurants, and a brochure for Montreal. Molly had never been to Montreal, but she'd heard it was a wonderful city.

Finally, the machine issued its last gasp. Molly retrieved her mug and sat at the counter with the others. Angus was already curled up near her stool.

"So when are you heading to Florida?" Molly asked. She wondered if the police were finished with their inquiries yet. She doubted it. And what about funeral arrangements?

Sheila ran a hand through her hair. "Oh, pretty soon. Once the police tell me I can leave town." She tried to laugh but it fell flat.

Molly changed course. "I know it's a delicate subject, but have you planned a service for Sheldon yet?" Surely no widow would leave town before that happened. "We'll be happy to help plan it, if you need us." She sipped her drink.

Sheila's cheeks reddened. "I'm not having a service." Her

tone was tense, almost harsh. "Sheldon will be cremated. I prefer something private."

"That's understandable," Carol said in a soothing voice. "Many people do."

Sheila traced a gold vein in the granite counter with her finger. "At least he left me well provided for. One benefit of being married to an insurance man."

Molly imagined that the couple probably had huge life insurance policies. Although money was no substitute for someone you loved, she was sure having it was far better than being broke. "Will you keep the business going?"

"How can I?" Sheila frowned. "I'm not licensed to sell insurance. Sheldon never wanted me to be, even though we didn't make nearly as much money as Sheldon wanted everyone to think when he talked me into buying this fancy house. The existing policies we have with customers will be reassigned to other agents."

"I always wondered how that worked," Molly said. Evading Sheila's gaze, she focused instead on the shed in the backyard, noticing spiky-leafed bushes lining one wall. "What's that cute little building out there? And what are those bushes?" They seemed familiar, but Molly couldn't remember what they were called.

Sheila turned on her stool to peer out the window. "That's my art cabin, where I create my masterpieces." She narrowed her eyes, as though squinting across the space. "And those are pink and white rhododendrons."

"They must be so pretty when they're blooming," Molly said. "And it's wonderful that you have your own space to work."

"Sheldon insisted," Sheila said. "I need the privacy in order to create. Many artists do."

"I love rhododendrons," Carol said. "But we had to pull ours out because the neighbor's dog took a liking to them. They're poisonous."

"Oh yes, I've heard that," Molly said. "So many plants are poisonous to pets. You have to be careful. Anyway, I love your cabin."

"I'll take you out to see it if you want," Sheila said. Perhaps sensing hesitation, she added, "No one has seen it yet, except Sheldon of course. And I always dreamed of sharing it with friends."

How could they say no? "That sounds nice," Molly said. "After we finish our coffee, we can pop out there." Then she remembered Tara. What if she was skulking in the woods, waiting to pounce?

Carol must have had the same thought because she craned her neck to peek out the window. "Have you seen anyone lurking around your property today, Sheila? Or had any visitors?"

Sheila, who had just taken a mouthful of coffee, sputtered, sending droplets of liquid flying. "What are you talking about?" she asked, dabbing the countertop with a napkin. Fear crept into her eyes. "You mean, someone who is after *me*?" She slid down from her stool and rushed to the window. "No, I haven't seen a soul aside from you two."

Molly went to stand beside her. Except for the shoveled path to the shed, the snow in the backyard was an unbroken expanse of white. She didn't even see any animal tracks. "Phew. I don't see any footprints."

Sheila's fists were clenched. "Whose footprints?"

"Tara Taggart's," Molly said bluntly. "The police are searching for her. They think she killed Finlay."

Sheila's mouth dropped open. "That little *mouse* is the killer?"

"Or her son, maybe," Molly said. "According to the police." She really didn't want to give Sheila the details of the case against the Taggarts or talk about the Bakehouse Three's involvement.

"I really doubt Tara would come here," Sheila said, returning to her stool. She tossed her head with a scoffing sound. "I barely know her."

But Tara knew your husband. "Well, she's wandering around in the cold," Molly said, returning to the counter. "So if she does seek shelter here, call the police immediately."

"You bet I will." Sheila pressed her lips together. "Maybe she killed my Sheldon too."

"Why would she do that?" Carol asked innocently. "Did they know each other?"

An ugly red flush stained Sheila's neck. "Yes," she practically spat. "They dated each other decades ago, long before we got married. I came across some messages they sent each other recently on social media—things a wife should never find."

"Oh my," Carol said. "That is unpleasant."

Sheila's fingers tightened around her mug. "Maybe she killed Sheldon." Then, as if a switch was flipped, she set the cup down with a thud. "Let's go see the shed, shall we?"

"Sure," Carol agreed. "Then Molly and I ought to get back to town."

Sheila stood, pointing at a pair of French doors leading to the deck. "I'll meet you there in a minute. I left my coat in my bedroom."

Molly and Carol put their mugs in the sink, then retrieved their coats and boots and carried them to the back door to avoid getting any melted snow on the floor. While they donned their outdoor gear, Angus danced around, eager to go outside. He was the only one who was excited, Molly observed wryly. She was already wincing against the blast of cold air waiting to greet them.

Sheila bustled back into the kitchen, dressed in a puffy down jacket with a fur-lined hood. She pulled up the hood and slid on a pair of gloves, then pushed her feet into boots. "Ready?"

"Sure," Carol said, reaching for the door handle.

The three women and the dog made their way across the deck and down a flight of stairs to the yard. Sheila charged ahead to the shed. Angus wanted to sniff around, so Molly took her time, scanning the surrounding woods for any sign of Tara. But all was silent, the forest dark and deep as the sun lowered.

The building was basically one big room lit by skylights. Along three walls stood tables and shelves filled with art supplies. Rows of paintings were lined up on the wall and one in progress stood on an easel.

Molly tilted her head as she viewed it. Red and purple swirls filled the bottom half, while wavy, dark shapes lined the top.

"I'm calling it *Reflected Sunset on the Loch*," Sheila said with pride. "What do you think?"

"It's very evocative," Molly said, now seeing that the swirls were clouds and the wavy shapes suggested hills. Carol chimed in with something vague about the brushwork.

Angus whined at Molly's feet. At first, she fancied that he was also expressing an opinion about the piece.

But then she noticed that Sheila was aiming a gun at her.

20

Molly released a yelp of surprise. "Sheila, what are you doing?"

Carol spun around and gasped. She moved closer to Molly, bumping shoulders.

Sheila's features twisted into a sneer. "Don't play dumb with me, ladies. You know what you said." She curled one hand and gestured. "Give me those cell phones. Now."

Molly reached into her pocket, moving as slowly as she dared. She knew that once they gave up their phones, they were at Sheila's mercy. No one knew they were here—unless someone spotted her car.

As if reading her mind, Sheila wiggled her fingers. "And the keys. Good thing we have a nice big garage, isn't it?"

Oh no. Molly slid her gaze to Carol, who stood frozen, only the flicker of her eyelashes revealing her terror.

"I don't get it," Molly said. "Honestly, Sheila. What did we do? We only came over here to see how you were doing. And to warn you about Tara."

Sheila laughed. "Oh, boo-hoo. You two are so *good,* it's sickening. My husband was a jerk who convinced me to buy a house without telling me it was down the road from his old girlfriend. What makes you think I need *comfort*?"

Because you played the sympathy card so well? Molly knew better than to say that, but then she found herself blurting something worse. "You killed him, didn't you?" Now it all made sense, the attempted diversion when Sheila played the victim and forged a threatening note, the packed SUV, and now the gun.

Sheila's answer was to wave the firearm a little. "Phones, girls. I need them. Now."

Carol pulled hers out and set it gently on the floor. Molly removed hers from her pocket but didn't let go. It was as if her fingers were glued to it. "Honestly, Sheila, we never suspected you. What made you think we did?"

Sheila bent and picked up Carol's phone then tucked it into her pocket. "You talked about the bushes."

Oh. The dangerous rhododendrons. Sheila had poisoned her husband. "But when? How?" Molly didn't know much about that particular poison.

"Pretty clever of me, wasn't it?" Sheila couldn't hold back a grin. "I fed it to him the afternoon of the event. It takes a few hours to work, so I had to time it carefully. And everything went according to plan. He got sick while we were at the dinner."

"And since the McCauleys had provided the food, you thought Brodie would be blamed," Carol said, her voice heavy with anger and disgust.

Sheila laughed, a grating sound. "Of course. The first murder gave me the idea. Oh, I'd toyed with the idea of bumping off dear old Sheldon for a while. Especially after he reconnected with Tara. Why should I let him divorce me and give me a pittance when I could get a cool million or two in life insurance? And better yet, never have to see his ugly mug again."

Her voice held so much spite that Angus whined. *Angus.* Molly couldn't let anything happen to him. "Will you please let Angus go? He never did anything to you."

Sheila studied the small dog huddled close to Molly's ankle. After a long moment, she shook her head. "Nope. He's always with you, so if I let him go, someone will figure out something's wrong."

"They will anyway, sooner or later," Carol said, clenching her fists. "I have a husband. And we have friends, family. People are going to notice."

The other woman's eyes narrowed. "But I'll be long gone. So good luck." She pointed at Molly. "Phone. Keys. Now."

Molly ever so slowly took the phone out of her pocket and placed it on the floor. There went her lifeline. Next she found the keys and put them beside the phone, then scooted them across the floor toward Sheila.

How were they going to get out of here? They'd have to break the door down since there wasn't any other way to exit unless they climbed to the skylights twelve feet overhead.

Molly gulped in air, trying to slow her racing heart. At least it was heated in here. And Sheila hadn't shot them. They were healthy and warm. That would have to do for now, until they figured a way out of this jam. She certainly didn't plan to sit here and wait for someone to find them. That might take days.

"Sheila?" a woman's voice shouted from outside. "Sheila, where are you?"

Sheila's eyes widened. "Tara," she hissed. She snatched up Molly's phone and keys and shoved them into her pocket. "You aren't going anywhere, so get used to it." She backed toward the exit, the gun leveled at them until she disappeared through the door.

"We'll be able to get out," Carol whispered once Sheila was gone. "We can unlock the handle from inside. We don't need a key."

Molly studied the door, which looked like every other modern door. Then she heard another sound. Running closer, she listened carefully. From the scraping sounds, she guessed that Sheila had padlocked them in. And when she pushed on it a moment later, she discovered her theory was right.

"We are trapped," she told Carol. "She padlocked the door." Angus yipped and bolted to the door, then scratched it frantically. "I'm sorry, boy. We can't get out."

Carol hugged herself. "I wonder what's going on with Tara and Sheila."

"You mean, who will kill whom first?" Molly asked wryly. If only she could see outside. She scanned the room. One wooden table with sturdy legs was well placed under a row of windows. Molly pushed aside jars of paint and other supplies and climbed up.

Carol came closer and watched as Molly stood up on the table, got her balance, and went to the narrow window.

She had to stand on tiptoes, but she got a good view of the backyard. Sheila was walking around in the snow, still holding the gun, but Tara was nowhere to be seen. "I think Tara is hiding," she reported to Carol.

"Good idea, since Sheila is armed." Carol tipped her head and gazed up at Molly. "I don't suppose you can climb out one of those windows?"

Molly didn't even have to assess the window to answer. "I'm afraid not. I'll never fit through."

"Too bad we can't put Angus through," Carol said. "At least we could set him free."

"The drop is too far," Molly said. "He might get hurt. Besides, I'd be afraid Sheila or Tara might intercept him and . . ." She couldn't finish the thought. Instead, she climbed down off the table and glanced around. She pointed to two doors at the rear. "Let's check those."

"Good idea," Carol agreed.

Molly opened the first door and found a closet stuffed full of junk. No chance of escape through there. She crossed the short distance to the other door and pushed it open, revealing a tiny bathroom with a sink, toilet, and shower stall. There was a small window at eye level, but it was too small for Molly or Carol to fit through.

Molly felt a sudden gust of cold air and rubbed her arms. "Brr."

Angus apparently felt the air as well, because he rushed in and wiggled his way behind the toilet.

"Angus, what is it?" Molly asked, crouching down to see what had drawn his attention. But before she had a chance to register what was happening, Angus had vanished. "Angus!"

"What's the matter?" Carol asked, alarm coursing through her tone.

Speechless, Molly peered around the base of the toilet and saw that a vent cover had come detached from an opening—and Angus had squeezed his way through without a second thought. "He's gone," she said, barely believing it.

"He must have sensed we need help," Carol said firmly. "He's such a brave little guy."

Molly pressed her face to the window, searching for a sign of Angus. As she did, a gun went off, the sound echoing around the hillsides and woods. With a shiver, Molly hoped Sheila hadn't shot someone.

"That will draw attention," Carol said, urgency in her voice as she joined Molly at the window. "Someone will investigate the shot. Or Angus will find somebody. We'll be okay, Molly." She pointed. "Look, there he is."

Angus was just disappearing into the woods lining the property. Right beyond that band of trees was the main road. Molly sent up a prayer that he'd stay safely away from danger.

Movement caught her eye, and she quickly ducked out of sight. What was going on out there? Would anyone call the police after hearing the gunshot? Hopefully people wouldn't think it was target practice or a hunter.

Carol filled a clean paper cup with water and drank it down. "For being in captivity, this isn't too bad."

Carol was clearly being droll to help diffuse the gravity of the situation. The comment struck Molly hard, and she burst into giggles.

After the laughter ebbed, tears welled. Molly imagined Angus trotting down the road, tags jingling, looking for a friend, and a sense of helplessness constricted her heart. Oh, how she loved that dog. She sobbed, wiping her eyes and nose with a tissue Carol handed her from a box in the bathroom.

"It's going to be all right, Molly." Carol rubbed Molly's back reassuringly, her voice calm and soothing. "I refuse to allow any other possibility into my mind."

Molly blew her nose. "I know. Just a stress reaction, I think."

Someone fumbled at the lock outside. Carol and Molly stared at each other with wide eyes for a moment before Molly burst into action. There was no way she would allow Sheila to bully them further. Absolutely not.

Moving as quietly as possible, she picked up a ball of twine and quickly unraveled several feet. She handed the loose end to Carol and pointed to a position on one side of the door. "Hold it taut a few inches above the floor," she whispered.

Carol frowned skeptically but took the twine. "Are you sure this will work?"

"No, but it's worth a try." Molly moved into a spot across from Carol. With luck, Sheila would enter the shed in a hurry and not notice the trip wire at ground level.

The knob rattled and then the door swung open. A female figure silhouetted against the brighter snow paused for a second before rushing over the threshold.

Molly felt the twine ball jerk in her hand but she held it firm, and the woman fell to the ground with a grunt of surprise. As she hit the floor, Molly realized in shock that the newcomer wasn't Sheila after all.

21

Tara Taggart crashed to the floor like a felled tree, and the gun she held went skittering across the floor with a clatter. She banged her head on the floor and didn't move.

"Where's Sheila?" Molly and Carol asked each other in unison. Seeing a more pressing matter, Molly scooped up the gun.

Carol checked to make sure Tara was breathing, then wrapped some twine around her wrists and ankles. "I don't want to tie it too tight, but this will at least slow her down."

"Check if she has a phone," Molly suggested.

Carol patted Tara's coat pockets. She removed a phone from one and handed it to Molly by the edges. "It might be locked."

Molly took the phone and touched the screen. She felt a shiver of relief when it came on. "Not locked." She had never dialed 911 so quickly in her life. When the dispatcher answered, she said, "This is Molly Ferris. Carol MacCallan and I have apprehended the fugitive Tara Taggart in Sheila Barker's shed. She needs medical attention."

"What kind of medical attention?"

Molly glanced at Carol. "She fell down and hit her head. Speaking of which, there's another woman who needs to be apprehended. Sheila Barker. She confessed to the murder of her husband and locked us in a shed. But we're out now, and we have her gun, so we don't think she's armed anymore."

"You've been busy. I'll send the police and an ambulance. Stay where you are."

Molly disconnected. "No, we are not staying where we are. Not until we're sure Sheila isn't coming back here. Besides, I need to find my dog."

"Tara had her keys," Carol said, pointing to the padlock where they still hung. "So that doesn't bode well for Sheila. What if she was shot?"

Molly tugged the keys out of the lock, recalling the gunshot they heard. "Why don't we go find out?"

Tara rolled around on the floor, groaning and struggling to get loose. Seeing that she was okay, Molly felt a little better about leaving her in the shed. With Sheila's whereabouts unknown, it was for her own safety as well as theirs.

"Are you sure about this?" Carol asked as Molly hooked the padlock over the hasp. "Shouldn't we wait here for the police?"

"We could," Molly said. "But what if Sheila is injured? She may be a murderer, but I'd like to see her stand trial." She inhaled sharply, forcing her mind away from possible scenarios.

"You're right," Carol said. "At least this time we're not going to walk into a trap."

"No, we aren't." Molly scanned the property, then pointed into the woods. "I think the gunshot came from over there."

They waded through the snow, passing by the house. Molly didn't see any signs of activity inside the kitchen. The lights over the island where they'd been sitting still glowed.

Until they reached the woods, the snow was unbroken. But on its fringe, they spotted an area that had been trampled. Molly studied the footprints closely. "I think Tara and Sheila made these prints."

Carol bent closer. "You're right. See the two different boot treads? It looks like they were fighting."

Molly stepped into the woods. She didn't spot any blood, thank goodness. Maybe the shot hadn't hit anyone. But where was Sheila now?

When she returned to Carol, her friend pointed to two sets of footprints leading back toward the house. "I think they went that way."

Careful not to step in the tracks, Molly and Carol followed them around the house to the driveway, which was clear enough of snow that they vanished. Molly's car was missing, but the SUV was still parked in the same spot in front of the garage.

Molly peered through the garage windows and saw her car inside. "Sheila hid my car in there. She's got to still be around somewhere."

Carol used a gloved hand to open the SUV's front passenger door. "The key fob is on the console," she said. "Why didn't Tara drive away in Sheila's car?"

Instead, she had taken Sheila's shed keys and come out back. Molly's heart sank. "Maybe she was trying to help us. Let us go."

"Or not." Carol folded her arms. "We're witnesses, remember? She had Sheila's gun."

"True." Thinking of a possibility, Molly went to the SUV and opened the driver's door, careful as Carol had been not to leave prints. Feeling a jolt of triumph, she spotted the garage door opener clipped to the visor. Molly pressed the button and the garage door rose slowly, the mechanism whirring. Lights overhead came on, glaring down on Molly's car and revealing shelves and workbenches at the rear.

Molly edged around the far side of her car and found Sheila lying on the concrete floor, hands and feet bound. She was also gagged for good measure, with a none-too-clean cloth. She lifted her head slightly and stared at them with urgent eyes, mumbling behind the gag.

Molly bent to remove the gag. "Are you all right?" she asked.

Sheila's response was a growl. "Untie me. Let me up." She rolled from side to side, straining at her bonds. She didn't appear to have any injuries, Molly noted with relief.

"I don't think so," Carol said. "You can wait right there until the police come, which should be any minute."

"What happened with you and Tara?" Molly asked. "Did you fight? I take it she won."

"That woman," Sheila growled. "She tackled me. And then took my gun away." Her eyes narrowed. "Where is she? And how did you two get out?"

"Oh, she's kind of tied up at the moment," Carol said "She came to the shed—why, we're not exactly sure—and we were able to overpower her."

"I begged her not to touch my paintings in the shed when she took my keys," Sheila said, fury in her eyes. "But I guess she's not a good listener."

Molly was grateful Tara hadn't obeyed Sheila. Likely, Sheila had just piqued Tara's curiosity by mentioning the shed, and Tara had decided to see what she had hidden inside.

Molly glanced toward the road. Was that the faint sound of sirens she heard? And where was Angus? Still trotting along alone, or had he found someone? As soon as the police got here, she was going to go search for him.

"You two think you are so smart," Sheila said. "I knew I should have taken care of you while I had the chance."

That comment inflamed Molly. She pulled out Tara's phone and pushed the record button. "Why don't you say that again, Sheila? I'm sure the police will want to hear your threats."

Naturally Sheila subsided into silence with a mutter. There was nothing more they could do at the moment, so Molly and Carol stepped back into the driveway to wait. Soon lights flashed through the trees, and a convoy rumbled up the drive, consisting of three cruisers, an ambulance, and Fergus's Range Rover.

Once the vehicles were parked, Chief Thomson hopped out of the first cruiser, and the women rushed to greet him. "Of course it's you two. Are you all right?"

"We are, Chief," Molly said.

Carol nodded. "Not a scratch."

Harvey emerged from the Range Rover's passenger side, and Fergus started to climb out of the driver's side. But then a black, furry blur pushed past Fergus and bolted toward Molly.

"Angus!" Molly cried. She scooped up her wriggling dog and allowed him to give her kisses. "Good boy."

Fergus walked up, followed by Harvey. "Angus came down to the loch and headed right for me," Fergus explained. "When we heard the sirens, we kind of figured you were involved, so we followed the flashing lights." He hugged Molly while Harvey clung to his wife, scolding her quietly.

"All right, Chief, we're ready to talk," Molly said. "Tara Taggart is in the back shed." She dug for the keys and handed them to another officer. "She's locked in and she has a head injury."

Carol took over, pivoting to face the open garage. "And in there you will find Sheila Barker under restraint, thanks to Tara. Before she locked us in the shed, Sheila confessed to us that she killed her husband, using poison from her rhododendron bushes."

"I'm so glad we got rid of ours," Harvey muttered.

"I look forward to hearing the full story here." The chief barked orders to his team. The officer with the keys led the paramedics to the shed. Two other officers went to talk to Sheila. "And we'll get the crime scene team here ASAP," he said. "We've got unlawful restraint and assault charges to process."

Carol blanched. "I'm sorry Tara hit her head when we tripped her. We thought she was Sheila, coming in to shoot us."

"It was my idea," Molly said, panic tingeing her voice. "And Tara was armed with Sheila's gun." She put Angus down and patted her coat pocket. "The gun is right here. We had to tie Tara up so she wouldn't escape."

"Take the gun into evidence," the chief ordered an officer. He leveled his gaze at Molly and Carol. "Regarding the assault charges . . . I wasn't talking about you ladies. You helped apprehend not one but two criminals. I don't want to arrest you, but I do want a full statement."

Molly's shoulders slumped in relief. She carefully handed the officer the gun. "I'm glad to hear that. Where and when do we give our statements, Chief?"

He eyed the women, no doubt realizing how exhausted they were. "Why don't you wait in one of the vehicles for a few minutes, then we'll talk a little more. I want the basics now, but we can do longer, more formal statements tomorrow."

Fergus stepped forward. "They can wait in my car, Chief. It's nice and warm, plus I've got hot coffee and cookies."

"That sounds heavenly," Molly admitted.

"Fine by me." Carol rested heavily on Harvey. "I can't wait to sit down."

Harvey and Carol climbed into the back seat, and Molly got in front with Fergus. Angus curled up in Molly's lap to doze, clearly relieved to be reunited with her. Fergus unzipped an insulated bag and withdrew a thermos of coffee. Molly held the cups while he poured, then handed them back to Harvey and Carol. Hers and Fergus's went into the cup holders.

They all sat in silence, soaking up the peace inside the Range Rover. In contrast, outside the car, the officials were doing their work—EMTs loaded Tara into an ambulance, a handcuffed Sheila was guided into a cruiser, and officers flowed in and out of the house as they searched for and gathered evidence.

Fergus finally broke the silence. "You solved two murders in one go today. Well done, ladies."

"I'm very impressed," Harvey said. "It's obvious to me who has the brains in the MacCallan household."

"Oh honey," Carol said, leaning on Harvey's shoulder. "You tell the sweetest lies."

Molly was warmed by the men's praise, but honesty compelled her to say, "It was all kind of an accident, with one thing leading to another. We only came over here to warn Sheila about Tara."

"You see, Tara and Sheldon dated years ago, before his marriage," Carol said. "So we thought Tara might have unfinished business with his wife."

"We even thought that Tara might have killed Sheldon by accident," Molly said. "Or on purpose. We weren't sure."

"It sounds complicated," Fergus commented.

"Oh it is," Molly said. "I'm still wrapping my head around the details. At first we thought there was only one killer, and we were trying to find the connections between the two deaths. Tara knew Sheldon, and so did Brodie. Sheila claiming to be the intended victim only muddied the waters."

"As she intended," Carol said. "I think she saw her chance to get rid of Sheldon when Finlay was killed. She was hoping that Brodie would take the rap for that one as well."

Fergus glanced at the white SUV, piled with belongings. "Was Sheila planning to make a run for it? Appears that way." He handed around a plastic container filled with chocolate chip cookies.

"Oh yeah." Molly took a cookie and bit into it with extra appreciation for the warm, soft treat. "She was talking to us about going to Florida, but I saw a brochure for Montreal on her refrigerator. She was probably trying to mislead us."

"And I'll bet Tara wanted to steal that SUV," Carol said. "That's what I would have done if I were her. She could have been in Canada before anyone even realized the car was stolen."

Molly swallowed a bite of cookie. "I think you're right. She was probably going to use Sheila's identification. Both are about the same height and weight with a similar hair color."

Harvey leaned forward and tapped Fergus on the shoulder. "See why I can never get away with anything? My wife can run rings around me."

They all laughed. Molly took a deep breath, probably her first truly relaxing one since this ordeal had begun. But now it was over, they all were safe, and she could unwind with her loved ones and celebrate the future. In fact, they had a fun celebration to prepare for in the very near future.

"So, Carol, tell me." She angled to face her friend, who raised her eyebrows. "What are you wearing tonight for the final Robert Burns supper at King's Heid Pub?"

22

Brodie and Catriona were the first people Molly saw when she entered King's Heid Pub that evening. The couple wore traditional Scottish dress featuring a gorgeous black-and-green McCauley tartan. Behind them, one of the huge fireplaces roared, sending out waves of heat. A quartet softly played folk songs in the corner and guests were circulating, chatting before the meal began.

"Molly!" Catriona cried, holding out her arms. Her curly hair was piled high, tendrils escaping to dangle on her neck. "How can we ever thank you?"

Molly returned Catriona's hug, then Brodie's. "No thanks needed. We couldn't stand by and let you get blamed for something you didn't do," she said truthfully.

Brodie's handsome face was somber. "I'm so glad you had faith in me. I know the police were just doing their job."

Catriona tossed her head. "They were only following the bread crumbs Tara left for them. What a devious woman."

Molly couldn't disagree. "We were shocked when we realized it was her," she said as she waved over Carol, Harvey, and Laura, who had just entered the room. "Actually, Angus is the one who broke the case. He found her night vision goggles."

After Tara had recovered in the hospital, which didn't take long since she was only stunned, not seriously injured, she'd given a full confession—which, of course, had filtered quickly through the Loch Mallaig grapevine. Upon learning that Finlay Croft was going to be in town, she'd watched for a chance to kill him. Tara had noticed—and admired—the bow and arrows in the Neeps and Tatties office while visiting her son during one of his shifts. When she learned that Finlay was going to the Robert Burns supper along with other possible suspects, she decided the perfect opportunity had arisen. Since she wasn't attending the dinner, she wouldn't even be on the initial list of suspects. And the murder would even be a little ironic. Imagine a Scottish literature professor being killed with a reference to a Robert Burns poem.

After slipping inside while everyone was focused on the haggis presentation to steal Brodie's bow and arrows, easily accessible to all the suspects present, she put on her goggles and lurked in the parking lot waiting for the professor to come out.

But when she saw Brodie leave to go to his house that evening, she decided to take things a step further and frame him. She planned to leave the equipment on his porch, but Brodie was in such a rush that he'd left the house unlocked, so she slipped in and left it in the hallway, with no one the wiser.

A couple days later, having heard that Molly and her friends were trying to exonerate Brodie, Tara had snuck into Neeps and Tatties during Brodie's homecoming celebration to try and eavesdrop. Becoming enraged when she learned whom they suspected in Finlay's murder, she'd stormed out of the restaurant and fled. Unfortunately, Tara had never guessed that any of them would ever visit her at home, so she hadn't gotten rid of the incriminating goggles.

Upon Tara's arrest, Jeanne Dupont was no longer a person of interest, and she had immediately returned to Marquette. Her Loch Mallaig cabin was already on the market. A funeral for Finlay Croft would be held at the college in a week or so.

Molly smiled as her friends approached. Carol and Laura also looked lovely in Scottish formal wear. Harvey was handsome in a kilt, his authentic Scottish tam-o'-shanter perched jauntily on his head.

"Good evening," Carol said. "How are you doing?" She and Laura exchanged hugs with Catriona, while Harvey gave Brodie a hearty clap on the back and vigorously shook his hand.

"And how's Noah?" Laura asked, concern in her voice. The young man had been devastated by his mother's arrest, although he had suspected her. He'd told the police that Tara had suffered from poor mental health and outbursts of anger. Brodie and Catriona had stepped forward to take him in, since he didn't want to stay at the cabin.

"He's doing better than we expected," Catriona said. "I think a big part of him is relieved. He'd sensed that his mother was headed toward another breakdown, but he didn't know what to do about it."

"I'm glad he has you to lean on," Molly said with sincerity. Every young person needed support and encouragement as they stepped into full adulthood. "It's big of you to take him in when his mother tried to frame you for murder."

"That was her choice, not his," Catriona said firmly. "He's a young man who needs help, and we can provide it, so we will."

"Is he still going to go back to college?" Laura asked.

Brodie nodded. "He is. And during this whole process, we learned more about what happened at Barrie-Firth. Another student cheated by stealing work from Noah, but Finlay blamed Noah. The other student is from a wealthy family who made a big donation to the college."

Poor Noah. He'd certainly suffered from serious setbacks in his short life. And now he faced another. "Can anything be done about it?" Molly asked.

Brodie smiled. "We're going to reopen the case with the college. Noah won't return there, but at least his record can be cleared." His grin widened. "Noah has proof, you see. Finlay didn't want to see it, and he used his clout to make Noah back down."

"That's awful," Laura said, shaking her head. Then understanding flashed across her face. "I wonder how much that factored into Tara's anger."

"As a mother, I can assume probably a lot." Molly knew from experience how upset she'd gotten when Chloe faced unfair treatment. Finlay had also treated Tara horribly by firing her. So far, she hadn't been able to find a similar job and was working well below her experience level. Molly was sure that resentment about her failed career fueled Tara's anger as well. Not that any of that justified murder.

A server approached them holding a tray of cider, and they each selected a glass. After the server moved on, Catriona asked, "Is there any more news about Sheila?"

"I did not see that one coming," Brodie said. "I mean, she wasn't the friendliest person and she complained a lot, but wow. I can't believe she planned her husband's death like that."

"We were pretty surprised too," Molly said. "I made the mistake of mentioning the bushes around her painting shed, and that set her off."

Carol took up the story. "Everything was good until that point. She seemed to be soaking up support from us." She huffed derisively. "What a faker she was. She really put a lot of thought into poisoning Sheldon."

"Then tried to throw the police off by claiming she was the intended victim." Laura's tone was wry. "I don't know if they ever believed that, though."

Molly sipped her cider, which was tart and tasty. "But it was an effective smoke screen. Like Tara, she hoped someone else would be blamed—namely Brodie, who was fresh out on bail and had that slow insurance payout as a motive, albeit a flimsy one. And she themed the killing to a Burns poem, like Tara did, so that the police would think the murders had been committed by the same person."

Harvey let out a rueful chuckle. "I'm sure glad we stopped those murderous women when we did. There are a whole lot of other Burns poems to provide inspiration. They might have cut quite a swath through Loch Mallaig."

"So true," Laura said. "I never noticed that aspect of his work until we started to investigate." She craned her neck around, then said to Molly, "The Piping Yoopers are lining up in the hallway. Aren't you playing?"

Molly smiled. "Not tonight. I get to sit and enjoy dinner with you all." Alastair had suggested Molly take the evening off in consideration of her ordeal that day. She didn't mind the break, especially since she hadn't even picked up her bagpipes to practice since the last performance.

Grizela Duff bustled around the room, urging people to hush and sit since the dinner was going to begin shortly. Molly hadn't visited the appetizer table, so she hurried to grab something to nibble on. She loaded a plate with samples from the wonderful selection of imported Scottish cheeses and crackers, and added a small bunch of grapes for good measure.

The Bakehouse Three and their friends were seated in back, near the fireplace, and it was a perfect spot to watch the celebration. The quartet stopped playing and Grizela picked up a microphone. The crowd fell silent when she stood at the head of the room, as though trying to avoid one of her sharp-tongued lectures.

"Good evening, all," the librarian said in greeting. "Welcome to the last evening of our Burns Week. It's been quite an experience, hasn't it?" The audience replied with affirmations. "Despite the tragedy that has marred this event, I want to express gratitude for you all." Her gaze lingered on Brodie and Catriona. "The test of a community lies in how we treat those who find themselves facing trouble. And I want to say that, in my view, Loch Mallaig has passed with flying colors."

Everyone burst into cheers and shouts. Once the noise died down, Grizela went on, "Now I'd like you to please welcome our orator for tonight, Vernon Pennycook. I had to beg a little before he finally agreed." Everyone laughed. "He'll be reciting for us after The Piping Yoopers perform. But first, he's going to give us an update on the fishing derby."

Everyone clapped as Vernon Pennycook shambled to the front of the room, his scrawny frame engulfed in a kilt and sash. "Good evening. Let me assure you, I've been practicing hard ever since Grizela put the finger on me." He cleared his throat to more laughter. "As you know, we wrapped up the Jock McCauley Fishing Derby this afternoon. We had an excellent turnout and caught some record fish."

Vernon spent the next few minutes handing out an array of trophies to the tournament participants. When only a few plaques remained on the awards table, he announced, "I'm going to do something a little extra with some help from our host this evening, Fergus MacGregor." He paused for a moment while Fergus walked up to the podium, and Molly could practically feel the crowd's interest ramp up. "Thanks to the swift and expert action of some good men, a young fellow's life was saved." The applause was deafening in response to Vernon's announcement.

"What a nice idea," Molly murmured to Carol, who was seated beside her.

Vernon read the names of those who had helped to rescue Noah, and Fergus gave out the commendations with a handshake. Harvey and the visiting fishermen were among the recipients, and Molly saw Laura give Sam a thumbs-up. A final award went to Fergus for helping supervise the rescue efforts, with Vernon saying a few kind words about his quick thinking in sounding the alarm.

After the applause for Fergus died down and the resort owner returned to the back of the room where the rest of The Piping Yoopers stood, Vernon spoke again. "I have only one more thing to add. Like Grizela said, we're a community that stands ready to help, no matter what and no matter when. Makes me proud to call this place home." He inclined his head in a nod as the onlookers applauded.

Alastair gave the signal, and The Piping Yoopers began to play "Scotland the Brave" as they circled the big room once, then marched into formation at the front.

Molly's heart swelled as she listened to the song, which always touched her deeply. She glanced around the table at her friends, grateful to have them in her life. They might face trouble on occasion in Loch Mallaig, but with a little grace and faith, everything always turned out all right in the end.

Up to this point, we've been doing all the writing. Now it's *your* turn!

Tell us what you think about this book, the characters, the bad guy, or anything else you'd like to share with us about this series. We can't wait to hear from *you*!

Log on to give us your feedback at:
https://www.surveymonkey.com/r/ScottishBakehouse

Annie's FICTION

Victorian Mansion Flower Shop Mysteries™

Set on sparkling Puget Sound in the cozy island town of Turtle Cove, Washington, the stories in this enthralling series are good old-fashioned whodunits chock-full of fascinating family secrets, breathtaking scenery, heartwarming discoveries, and the unbreakable bonds of female friendships.

If you love the great outdoors, gardens, birds, flowers, and a good mystery book . . . then you'll love Annie's *Victorian Mansion Flower Shop Mysteries!*

AnniesFiction.com